Guy Inchbald was born in London, England in 1952 and has been moving around the country ever since. He went to more schools and universities than he can remember and has been at one time or another a trainee architect, student of philosophy, freelance designer, electronics engineer, parent, businessman, technical author, geometer, parish councillor and systems engineer, before turning to the writing of both fact and fiction. He is a Fellow of the Royal Society of Arts.

Nobody Steals My Air

And Other Stories

Guy Inchbald

steelpillow

Lulu

First published 2016
by steelpillow
in association with Lulu.com

Cover image by the author and Eric Rutten ©2016.
Model created by Eric Rutten.

Set in Palladio 10 pt font.

steelpillow, Park View, Queenhill,
Upton-on-Severn, Worcs. WR8 0RE, UK

ISBN 978-1-326-62387-6

To Haze, who brings me cups of tea
even when I don't deserve one.

Contents

Nobody Steals My Air

I had been away for a while, as they say, and I was going home.

Through the shuttle's window a small, bright dot grew larger, resolving itself into a hammer with a head at both ends, swinging in lazy arcs following each other round and round and glinting in the harsh sunlight of outer space as their black shadows chased each other across the monstrous orchid blossom of her solar array. *Effie III* was less than forty metres long and about as basic as a space station can get, but she was my home. The closer we got, the more my anticipation rose, I could feel my pulse beginning to quicken.

The airlock sidled along the main spar to the exact centre of rotation and de-spun itself as the hired shuttle craft approached. The craft drifted up to it and smoothly latched on without the slightest bump, just a faint "clunk-clunk" as the latches locked on.

I straightened up as the seat unclamped and grabbed my stuff.

"Thank you for travelling with Stellar Spaceways," the shuttle was burbling. "We hope you enjoyed your trip. Do you have any comment you would like to pass on? We are always trying to improve our ser...."

"Yeah, cut the crap," I replied curtly, pushing myself grumpily through the airlock as it opened with a slight hiss. "I told you not to spam me."

"I'm sorry, Sir. Goodbye."

The shuttle's platitudes cut off as the outer door closed. The same faint double-clunk signalled the shuttle's disengagement, and as it drifted away the airlock began to revolve around me, spinning itself back up to match Effie. I grabbed a handrail and let myself move with it as the inner door opened. Swinging into the main arm I began pushing myself feet-first along the ladder which ran from end to end inside. Gravity quickly made itself felt and I climbed down the rest of the ladder, growing steadily heavier, until at the bottom I was back to normal. Clambering down the last few rungs into the little living pod which formed one head of the hammer, I was home.

"Hi Effie," I called out to the air, "how's things?"

"Hi Jim. Welcome home, I've put the kettle on. No real problems. A couple of minor dust impacts to repair, and I did have to replace the water pump in the end but the 3D printer cartridge was within the budget you gave me, so I didn't bother to ping you."

I had asked Effie not to bother me with such trivia online, cybers can get so pedantic about these things.

"One thing just now though."

"Oh?"

"The airlock lost about half a cubic metre of air while it was open. Pressure in the shuttle was a tad low. It almost tripped my alarm."

"What! The two-faced bastards! Get me the most accurate estimate of how much you lost, what it was worth at that moment and lodge a formal complaint with the bank against Stellar!"

Any groundies reading this may not realise but it's an absolute rule in space, nobody steals another guy's air. It's like spitting in their face or having an affair with their partner – no, it's worse than that, it's like driving straight at them when they cross the road, it says you don't care if they lie down and die.

The scam that Stellar pulled on me is as old as space settling. Out here the most precious thing is stuff – any kind of stuff, there just isn't a lot of anything, that's what makes it space. You lose something, you could be a hundred thousand miles from getting another one. That makes it valuable.

And air is always on the lookout for a good leak. It's mardy stuff, air, it's no respecter of its owner's wishes, it just gets in there and pushes the laws of physics all the way. And leaks happen everywhere. A dust strike, an airlock door, a less-than-perfect seam on your space suit, your air will find it, and when it's found it, it's gone. Streaming out into space at hundreds of miles an hour, you'll never see it again. You won't live that long anyway. So air is especially valuable to us.

What could be easier than pumping down your airlock a little so that when you open the door it sucks in some of the other guy's air? I remembered now the faint hiss that had accompanied the opening of the shuttle's door. That goodbye schmooze hadn't really been spam, it was *meant* to irritate me, to distract me from the sound of my air being stolen. Well, actually, a lot of things could be easier. Modern spacecraft have every gadget imaginable to stop it happening – sensors, alarms, software accreditation, systems that monitor the monitoring systems. Bypassing all that ruck of technology is possible, but it ain't easy any more.

This wasn't just illegal, it would get Stellar blackballed by every settlement and station in the solar system.

The kettle hadn't even boiled before Effie came back to me.

"Jim, about that air. I got it audited. Stellar have lodged their official records and they show that no air has been transferred. The auditor says the encrypted monitoring records balance up, and the shuttle's systems all check out a hundred percent normal."

I sighed. "Thanks, Effie. Have the bank acknowledged the discrepancy between your records and theirs?"

"Yes, Jim. But you know how these things go. Who will they believe, the big commercial guy with all the money or the old lag stuck in a Type H?"

By "Type H" Effie meant herself. She was a Type H space station, the ones shaped like atwo-headed hammer and don't go all the way round in a wheel, the ones so small that some folks get sick from the varying gravity and can't live there, the ones that only low-life like me get left with. The other end? Oh, all the storage, power systems, fresh food tubs and the like, anything that can be shoved out there to counter-balance the weight of the living quarters.

We low-lifers especially guard our air like we guard nothing else. We have less than anybody and we can least afford to replace it. So we catch the space dust in aerogel, pump out the airlocks to distraction, check our suits like our lives depended on it – because they do. And one thing we do not like is for someone to come and steal it. You do that and word gets around, nobody will let you come close again, ever, you have to go Earthbound or suffocate. There are space settlements where it is legal to kill an air thief on sight, we care that much. I was born and bred in one of them, Ceres City we call it, though "city" is no more than an aspiration. These guys had not just stolen air worth half a day's pay to get it replaced, they had committed the most heinous insult that can be, a crime punishable by death.

I wasn't going out for blood – yet. Apart from anything else that would mean killing on Stellar's home ground, sure to be a place where it would be classed as murder. Bad boy I may be, but I ain't that bad. My own life was not at risk so killing in cold blood would be stretching the law even back in Ceres. But I was not going to take this lying down. And, although they had done a pretty good job of covering their tracks, something was nagging at me that this was about more than just a little smalltime theft. A spaceline is too big an operation to play dirty for peanuts. What was Stella's home ground?

"Earth," said Effie, "Their space-only operation is still new enough to price cheaply at a loss while it builds up, that's how they got your custom. Their main business is commercial traffic to the leo terminus stations: they are one of only two lines Earth will allow that close."

Of course, now I remembered. I had been so keen to get home, I had just grabbed the cheapest price without thinking. But an Earth based operation has less reason to steal air than most. The low-Earth-orbit "leo" stations are the cheapest places you can buy the stuff. No wonder something had felt wrong about the whole incident. There had to be something bigger behind it.

"Put me through to Ceres Protection, will you?"

Protection cover all kinds of unpleasantness. We are pretty much too small to have separate military and police hit squads and, truth be told, most of us don't see much distinction. Political borders are just empty talk when it comes down to it, a bad guy is a bad guy wherever he she or it comes from, and we deal with 'em all in just the same way – whatever it takes. That's Ceres Protection's job.

The kettle boiled while I was waiting so Effie set the tea brewing. Well, more precisely, one of the bots did. Not long after I bought Effie I had, ah, salvaged a couple of little bots to act as her hands, so she could be more active and independent of me in repairing herself and suchlike. They repaired each other too, I always loved watching that. Matter of fact, they did a good deal of that before they were usable, they had been pretty much scrap when I got hold of them. Somebody might have wanted them back otherwise. But that's another story.

Presently Effie put up a familiar face on the nearest screen in front of me. She hadn't found me just any policeman, she had gone not only to Ceres but to someone she knew would see my side of things, bless her.

"Sergeant Dodds, you old fraud! Still not cashiered. Got me any moonshine today?"

Kordja Dodds and I grew up together in Ceres, we were wild boys, he just calmed down when we eventually went our different ways.

"Why Jim, they haven't let you out again have they?" he grinned delightedly.

"Sure have. And they've done something else too. I want to file a criminal charge of air theft."

Kordja's expression changed. He let out a long, falling whistle. He must have been as shocked as he looked. I explained what had happened. Stellar made him whistle again.

"You betcha, Jimmy boy. Power consumption on the pumps, software maintenance log cycles, payments to the dark side, I'll get the Commissioner to sign a warrant – hey, here we go, he's awake this morning."

Kordja blinked, did a double-take.

"Well, look right here. Commissioner revokes his warrant pending allegations of police corruption laid by Stellar Spaceways. Jim, I'm afraid my hands are now tied. If you want to bring a prosecution you'll have to do it yourself. Still, anything we got done in those few seconds still stands. You wanna ask for the case notes before they get redacted?"

"I sure do."

"Oh crap, they've just been redacted."

Effie chipped in. "That's okay boys, I put in a legal demand to the police cyber myself and it passed them over before it got the redaction order. It is now asking for me to erase them, I'm going to break this connection before the Sergeant can make an enforceable demand in return, as he has just been ordered to do."

Kordja opened his mouth and drew breath to speak but no sound had time to escape before the screen blanked.

You begin to understand why I regard Effie not as some pokey little stinkbucket but as my home. She's no more comfortable to live in than the prison cell I had so recently left, but she sure knows how to look out for me. Why "Effie"? I don't know, I never got the chance to ask her previous owner and she won't talk about him. I bought her off a scrap dealer and cleaned her up. The filth was unbelievable, I won't mention the kitchen floor. Some people just get like that when they live alone. it was the cleaning cost that put the dealer off reselling her. Then I came along and grabbed a bargain in exchange for a little good honest sweat. Took me nearly a year of patient sorting, separating and rubbing down. But then, I had to do something while Effie zigzagged her way across the settlements to a promising asteroid I had in mind, and I could sell the recovered materials for a fair few bits as I went along: even a bucket of filth has value out here. I keep a clean house – for a red-neck, and

I like to think Effie appreciates it. Anyway, I'm getting off the subject.

Just ten minutes after boarding, I sat down and poured my first decent cup of tea for – well, far too long. The ability of Stellar's lawyers to strike so deep into even the Ceres political system was a shock to me. We are a pretty hard-line bunch when it comes to truth and openness among our bureaucrats and we don't take kindly to corruption. That charge against the Commissioner could not have been laid lightly. What's more, it would have to have been prepared in advance. Even today's cybers can't dig up high-profile dirt on demand, just like that. It was all beginning to look as if I might just have bumped into the outer moon of a very large planet, as they say.

Flipping through the police records, the evidence against Stellar was there to be gleaned all right. They had not only retrieved all the shuttle logs and Stellar's records, they had trawled in data from all the nearby cybers and their sensors: navigation requests and deviations, communications timing correlations, materiel deliveries, everything you could think of and plenty you never would, alongside the actual cyber logs, updates, backups and the like. Even for a police cyber it was an impressive haul for three seconds' worth of activity, never mind one that was all a two-bit frontier community of barely a thousand souls could put together, and I was duly impressed – and not a little proud.

In amongst it all were just the signs that I had hoped for. Net activity on a software link shortly before the activity logs were cycled and copies either lost or tampered with. Fuel burn records for the period after disengaging with Effie had been held in memory during a burst of cyber activity before being archived. Yes, fuel burns do allow the calculation of mass sensitively enough to detect the odd extra whiff of air. Everything definitive had either been destroyed or showed signs of tampering, but that in itself was indirect evidence and added to the pile. We had a case.

"Effie, could you connect to the Commissioner's home cyber on the systems net? You know, home-to-home chitchat? See if you can get a message in or ferret anything out?"

"I don't know, Jim. It's sure to be tapped and it won't dare accept the Tor or the Steg. I'd have to find some kind of proxy with a valid excuse to come calling. What about Ceres itself?" By this Effie meant the Ceres government cyber.

"Too risky again, we don't know how far in these clowns have gone."

"The Singularity?"

"Unh. You never know whose side it's on. Our forefathers came out here to get away from it, remember?"

"Okaaay. Here's another line. I have found a few Type H's open to tor-ing and stegging on our inter-system support link. We can't get onto the dark net proper from there, so right now we're all playing Kevin Bacon."

I knew what that meant, sort of. "Who the hell was Kevin Bacon anyway?" I asked abstractedly.

"A lousy twentieth-century actor who turned out to be connected to every movie star of the day in just six steps."

"Hunh. Is that for real or is it a Calvin's dad answer?" I felt secretly proud to find a contemporary allusion to go with Kevin Bacon.

"It's for real. And there's no need to be proud about Calvin's dad. Maybe I should set a bot into Hobbes mode."

These cybers, they sense everything. Eyes, heartbeat, hormones, everything. It's good to be looked after. Yes, it was indeed good to be home, but there were more important things on my mind. An old memory tugged at me.

"I have an old friend called Mishi Haylo. Once you guys have joined hands, can you rattle her cage? She's so far out they probably won't know to bug her."

"Do you have any contact details?"

"Nope. She just kinda disappeared."

"I'll have to find her first, then. Here goes nothing."

Mishi had been another Ceres kid of our generation. She had been a wild, untamed mind born to wild, untamed parents, leading on

Kordja and me into many a scrape. As kids we had been close for a while and I trusted her with my life. You know what kids get up to. Imagine all that in space suits – well, almost all that, for obvious reasons – and you can understand what I mean when I say that we trusted each other with our lives. At the age of sixteen, without warning and with barely a goodbye, she had inveigled her way onto some anonymous freighter and vanished off into the solar system. She had broken her silence only twice over the years, once when her first kid was born and she just had to tell the world, and again to show her online respects at her father's funeral. Her mother is still alive and has no more idea than I do what Mishi has been up to. I respected that silence and had never tried to call her back – until now.

Moments later, Effie said "Ow!" loudly and a red light started flashing. "Cyber attack," she blurted urgently. "If I come back just the same as now, don't trust me". The screen blanked, came back streaming lines of text up it – text for God's sake! Lights dimmed, flickered off and on. Gadgets around the place shut down and restarted. Something in the distance gave a muffled "thunk". The dreadful hissing of air into vacuum filled the cabin – the space cocks had opened! That was supposed to be impossible when anybody was on board. I was half way into my space suit when the hissing stopped abruptly and she called out again, "Hi, Jim, how do you like my new screen persona?" A bright green face stared out at me. "Different?" it asked, with an impish grin and a wink.

"Goddam, Effie, are you all right?"

"Just about. I'm afraid I have forgotten the last minute or so's system records. Didn't have time to squirrel those away, so they couldn't be trusted and I wiped them. Still not sure about the emergency service cyber, it doesn't like interruptions at the best of times. Or your suit for that matter. Would you mind stepping out of it?"

I did so, just in time to escape the worst of a disgusting stench that suddenly wafted out of it it.

"Recycler running in reverse," observed Effie. "How to kill a man with an overdose of farts."

The suit dropped to the floor, lay inert for a moment, then raised itself back up into its usual posture.

"Rebooted from a clean backup. If you can get over to the emergency batteries in the service pod and pull the power connector, I'll clean out the emergency cyber too."

That meant a short but stiff climb up to the middle and down the other side.

"Can't one of your bots go?"

"Not really, they have enough autonomy to cause trouble in their own right and I haven't got time to purge them. I've at least been able to deactivate them until I can deal with them properly."

"OK, I'll go," and I started up the ladder.

"Hang on, you ought to put the suit back on. Just in case."

I found myself so shaken up that I instinctively shied from the so recently lethal suit.

"No, do I really need to?"

"That is why I restored it first."

"Can't this wait for a bot?"

"I'd rather not. I am blocking the emergency cyber as a precaution and that is not a good long-term plan."

I sighed, suppressed the butterflies and stepped into the suit once more. The vile stench still clung faintly, and followed me all the way there and back. The only good thing about that climb in a space suit is that gravity fades as quickly as it arrives on the way down. Going down the other side is actually harder because the gravity rebuilds just as you are beginning to tire. And after so long in the slammer I tired easily. I resisted the usual temptation to let my feet go and slide down the handrail. It is just too dangerous when you're tired and slow because the rapidly-building gravity defeats your body's reflexes. I broke my ankles too many times as a kid to want to do so again just now. So I did it the slow way, sweating heavily into my warm padded clothing.

That's something else that groundies won't know. Huddled in a colony your body heat keeps everything lovely and warm: you even harvest the surplus heat energy to run the cooling system. Loners like me have the opposite problem: we get cold and keeping warm costs energy. Keeping the air just above freezing and wearing padded clothing saves us a lot of energy, it's part of our lifestyle.

I was recovering my breath at the bottom when Effie's voice came through in my helmet.

"Can you hurry up, Jim, I'm short on time."

The emergency batteries sat in a big rack in one corner. There were two duplicate power circuits as a fail-safe. It took me about thirty seconds to find the main output connectors and pull them. When I pulled the first one a speaker in the rack burst out at full volume, "STOP! DO NOT DISCONNECT THE EMERGENCY POWER!" A row of lights started flashing in patterns that made me feel queasy. I squeezed my eyes shut, felt for the second connector and pulled. There was a loud bang and a bright flash right through to the inside of my eyelids, then peace and quiet.

"Jim, are you all right?" Effie again.

"Yes, I'm fine. Are you?"

"Still smiling. Can you unclip the front panel just below the lights, you should see a couple of small metal pins over to the right."

"Yep."

"Can you put something across those pins to short them out?"

My toolbox was lying nearby. I took a small pair of tweezers and squeezed them across the pins.

"OK, now put everything back together."

I did as I was told. Lights came on, clunky things clunked, a whirry thing whirred briefly. "Hi, Jim," said the rack speaker. Then it all went quiet again.

"It's fine now. You can come back."

As I finally clambered out of the suit and discovered that my tea was now almost cold, the green avatar was still watching, now somewhat orange-tinted.

"Why the orange?"

"Ah, you noticed. Just my way of showing you how badly the emergency cyber got to me. There was a very nasty payload hidden in there. Besides attacking me directly it wound up the output to ten kilovolts, I only just held it off from the rest of the station. If you hadn't been in your suit you would have been electrocuted. And if you hadn't been so quick, I would have been, thanks for that."

"Is there any whisky left?" By now I was very severely shaken.

"All confiscated. But I made some vodka while you were away. It's the first half-litre out of the hot tap."

"Effie, you are a saint."

I drank cold tea laced with home made vodka and fell fast asleep in my own armchair. I had been home just thirty-five minutes.

When I woke up, Effie had the goods on Mishi. We couldn't talk direct, it had to be hidden deep in the cyber-to-cyber code exchange, home-to-home, slow but so universally abundant yet utterly mundane that nobody would look to any depth for dark traffic. Mishi would find out what she could and let us know. But, having lived in self-imposed exile for the last twenty years, that might not be very much. The police braindump was on its way over to her as fast as burying it in the service chatter could safely allow.

Turned out Mishi had joined the Freezone, a breakaway community of misfits who mistrusted any form of centralised government. More exactly, it was a loose federation of independent communities held together by mutual need. They did have common facilities, such trade and security outfits, but these were each run independently through community oversight and tended to be decentralised.

One of the things it meant was that it was even harder than usual to trace a human and their activity through the cybers: the core system network was deliberately made too dumb to know what was going on, its job was only to make sure that it *was* going on. Effie had had to locate Mishi by combing silently through the human social networking services and even then could not risk making direct contact, instead going indirectly through her station's routine support chit-chat.

Effie also had breakfast ready. Good old Effie, I was ravenous.

Then I sat down to think. Stellar, or whoever was behind them, would know that their lethal attack had failed and they would be sending something more physical along to finish the job. Effie was still sat in among the cloud of stations hanging off Mars One where she had been dumped after my arrest. Most probably they would try to arrange an "accidental" collision with some deadbeat hulk on its way to the scrapyard, but if they were desperate then it could be anything. I couldn't stay here, Effie couldn't stay here. But though we could and would run, we couldn't hide, at least not guaranteed, not if they could put the Ceres police out of action.

If I could get my evidence to Kordja, he would know who to pass it on to and blow the whole scam open. And that was exactly what they would be expecting me to try. No decoy tactics would work. The only thing I had on my side was the moment while they got organised, time was of the essence. I didn't have to get all the way to Ceres, just near enough to attract attention. The Ceres frontier guards were notoriously twitchy.

"Effie, get us to Ceres as fast as you can. Swing down."

This was going to be expensive. Effie fired little thrusters to slow down the spin that gave me my artificial gravity. It wouldn't stop entirely, but slowing it reduced the structural forces and allowed her to accelerate harder. At the same time she reeled in the gossamer-thin solar array, the orchid shrivelling back into its bud. As I grew slowly lighter, she fired the main engines and I found myself standing in a sharp valley as the floor swung up. A minute later and the wall and floor had swapped places. She still couldn't accelerate all that hard, so I didn't weigh much now. After an hour and a half she cut her engines altogether and, now featherweight, I stood once more on the floor proper. We needed to keep back enough fuel to stop when we got there.

I looked back anxiously at the star field behind us. Effie had a good scan. No sign of pursuit, thankfully. There was nothing to do now but pray it stayed that way, help the cleaned and rebooted bots tidy up the stuff that had fallen all over when gravity changed direction, and while away the next few weeks.

"Effie, have you got any verries I haven't seen?"

"Nope. I've still got those old movies if you are OK without virtual reality. Or you could buy something."

"Yeah, bring them up will you? Oh, and do I still have my springsuit?"

I had come across a cheap bunch of ancient movies – you know, flat-screen videos with sound and nothing else – shortly before I left for my "holiday" and had not had time to watch them. The idea of something so primitive had piqued my interest but, to tell you the truth, I had forgotten all about them.

I changed into my springsuit and, having not worn one for so long, fell to my knees like any greenhorn. I hate the things, the way they cling and the way they flip you around like a dog on a leash if you get off balance, but they keep your muscles fit during prolonged low-gravity. I pushed against it and stood up, my muscles remembering in seconds how to handle it. Then I sat down to watch a "movie". Get this, it was monochrome, not even coloured!

A few days later we heard on the news that the Ceres cyber had been attacked. It sounded just like the attack that Effie had beaten off, right down to the secondary infection of the emergency power system. Presently, an update said that the attacker had left traces in cyberspace and the trail was being followed. Next day they reported that the attacker had been identified and was now being hunted down.

OK, I was tired, I was just an old lag glad to be back home and with his own small troubles on his own small mind. But I should have guessed. To be honest, I don't know if it would have made a lot of difference, but I should have. And I needn't have run so hard either. Because the next move wasn't coming from behind.

Another week or so down the line, a ship coming the other way on the Mars run from Ceres changed course to intercept us. That made me nervous. Bright dots of light making the run would grow in the star field outside, flash past and disappear into the blackness as they showed their shadowed side. Suddenly one of them flared even brighter as its engines fired. They were powerful too, needing only twenty minutes to break its speed and reverse to match ours. That confused me. I knew only one kind of ship that carried such power, and it wasn't cheap liners.

"Jim, Ceres Protection want to talk to you."

What luck! This must be the frontier guard, right on the button. But why were they fingering me while still so far out? I took the call.

"James Dorville?"

"Yes, that's me. Hi there, bud."

"Stand by for boarding. Any sign of trouble from you or your station and we'll blow you out of the ether."

"What?! What 'n hell? Do you have a 'bad guy'?"

Before defending yourself, the one thing you have to be sure of is that the bad guy really is a bad guy and there ain't some little misunderstanding there. Unless they are under immediate threat, Protection need a 'bad guy' warrant before they can attack unprovoked.

"Sure do, buddy. You cain't go blasting Ceres cyber just 'cause it sent you down for a holiday. We'll be boarding in..." he paused, glanced sideways, "one minute thirty-seven."

Well, it was clear enough that there was a bad guy behind the attacks on Ceres, but I was not prepared for Protection to think it was me. Like I said, I really should have figured it out.

"Hold on there, Admiral, I'd like to lodge a formal misunderstanding."

"Just a Captain, buddy. That's what they all say. You got evidence?"

I raised a quizzical eyebrow at Effie's avatar.

"I'm sharing my comms logs with the ship cyber now. It says they have routing for the attacks that is supposed to trace back me but I don't have logs of any such comms. It says I could have purged them and can it search my personal memory to confirm?"

That would expose our conversations with Mishi to discovery. Much as it would clear my name, I couldn't allow the breach of trust. Of course, Protection would take my refusal as a sign of guilt.

I heaved a sigh. "You're safe, Effie, I can't allow that. Just let 'em in the door like a good housekeeper."

I started to strip off my springsuit, not without a certain sense of relief.

"Can you get my space suit ready?"

Presently the bright dot swelled to reveal itself as a neat little destroyer class, a battery of antennas, lasers and projectile guns aimed at us. A tiny shuttle boat detached itself and drifted across. I hurried to the airlock so it could spin down and stop, while the rest of Effie carried on her lazy turning. I wasn't going to take this lying down.

The gentle clunk-clunk of docking was quickly followed by the door opening. As the first suited body pulled itself through, gun-first, I slammed a wrench down on its wrist, pulled its legs through by the scruff of the neck and tugged on the lines of a cargo net that I kept handy, meanwhile Effie's bigger bot jerked forward hard and knocked back the barrel of the next gun that had been following just above his knees, she slammed the hatch shut, the bot pulling back to miss it by a neatly coordinated whisker, then she disengaged the shuttle and fired her own thrusters to turn away and aim for free space. It all happened so quick I felt it best to tell it all in one sentence, no drawing breath. She knew what my coded message "like a good housekeeper" had meant.

The captured suit had sergeant's stripes on it. I'd have dragged the other gunman through and taken him too, only Effie couldn't support more than two people for any length of time. My headset burst into life.

"Dorville! You tryin' to get yourself killed? You get back here!" The destroyer's captain was being rather predictable.

"Sorry, Captain. Your sergeant here is my hostage and if I go down, he goes down. You just keep tailin' me and maybe you can have him back in a while and not have to tell your Admiral how dumb you are. I won't hurt him 'less he earns it."

The boat and destroyer both moved to block our path but a Type H is small enough to turn on the spot quicker'n you can fly round it. Effie's main engine fired up, synchronising a slow and lumbering dance which kept them abeam. I raised my voice over the roar.

"I've been framed and one thing I learned is, it ain't easy to clear your name from inside a prison cell. I need to talk to someone on Ceres kind of unofficial. So here's the deal, Captain. If you can get my friend and me somewhere quiet for ten minutes, you can have Sarge back. Needs to be unofficial, so you'll have to brew up a cover story to get us together. And make sure it's quick because none of us has a lot of time. You can listen in all you like, 'cause it won't matter a politician's promise after that."

The Captain glared, saw the easy way ahead, nodded curtly. Effie cut the thrust to a trickle, turned back on course, cut it altogether.

I mean, why do all the hard work when you can get your opponent to do it for you? How in a hollow comet would I have ever gotten hold of Kordja on my own?

Dragging the net down to the cabin was a bit tricky. It was a big space suit, this guy must be tall. I left the poor soul's helmet on to protect his head from the bumps: he held his injured wrist protectively. Down there, I cracked it open, started in surprise. The face was part brown Asian, part white Western, much like mine, but with green-blue eyes and blonde hair and beard. It scowled back at me silently.

"Sorry about that, Sarge," I said conversationally. "I'd like to free that arm of yours so the doc can take a look at it. No funny business or I'll leave you to scream."

The bots helped me move the net over to the table, it was just as well the gravity was low. Effie swung the doctor down from the ceiling. I carefully cut a couple of strands of netting to allow the damaged wrist out, then began to gently remove the warmly padded glove. The face winced in pain.

"Doc, got any painkiller?"

Now it's a funny thing, but the human body does not heal major injuries well in zero-gee and nobody has ever found out why not. I got Effie to wind herself up again. While the Doctor was busy, I changed back into my springsuit and Effie put the kettle on.

Presently, a slightly ashen-faced Sergeant Mulhurri of the Ceres Protection Service sat comfortably tied in my spare chair, sipping tea with his free hand and discussing the finer points of teapot design with Effie. His gun lay in pieces in front of me, undergoing a good clean that it didn't really need but was an effective way of putting it out of action. The man was still a cop and he still had one good hand, I wasn't taking any chances.

"Ah," he was saying, "but the best teapot is not silver or china. The most perfect tea I ever drank was poured from an old aluminium pot. It was encrusted inside with the residues of a thousand brews from the most excellent of teas, it was only ever rinsed with clean water, never soaped or scoured, never! The glory of each new brew grew upon the glory of the last. The pot was renowned for it." He drifted into silence.

I caught his eye. "You might have used tasers, you bastards. Wasting my bloody air with this." I waved a bullet that would have gone straight through the cabin wall had it been fired.

"Your suit might have been armoured, you didn't need to fit through the hatch like we did." He had a point.

I realised it might be better to turn the conversation to safer lines. "Your ancestors European or American?" I asked, more conversationally. Our many cultural heritages are quite a social topic on Ceres. It helps us to sanity-check a society that is still too new and raw to be accepted without question, to steer it along chosen and tested paths rather than let it continue to evolve randomly as it did at first. Or so I am told. Anyway, it seems the opposite is the habit on Earth, where past differences are still an embarrassment to the communal memory.

"Indian like you, my dark-haired Mr. Dorville. I am Kalasha, descendant of Alexander the Great. My great grandparents had tea plantations. Even cybers cannot grow tea as it should be grown, any more than they can serve it." He scowled at my own battered steel teapot. "And apricots. Do you have apricots by any chance? A good apricot is food of the Gods, ah. Protection does not approve of apricots on its ships, the stones are too hard to recycle." He scowled again. "And you, Mr. Dorville, where do your ancestors originate?"

"Call me Jim. Nepal, with a good dose of British – I am half Gurkha, half British shopkeeper."

We neither of us needed to explain more. Our ancestral homelands lay in among the same great sweep of mountain ranges, mine in the Himalaya and his over to the west in the Karakorum, ruled over by Mt. Everest's great rival, Nanga Parbart.

A slow grin replaced Mulhurri's scowl. "Then let the half Gurkha have half an apricot, it can wait no longer and must be eaten today," and Mulhurri produced a small bag from an inside pocket, rolling out onto the table one last lone perfect, magnificently ripe and fragrant apricot, which he got Effie to cut in half. "I brought it with me in the hope of leaving the stone behind," he explained with a wink.

"Sure, Effie can recycle worse than that," I replied amiably.

"Ah!" Mulhurri's eyes gleamed. "Would you mind...?" and he indicated another pocket that he could reach only with his useless hand. I ferreted in there and brought out another bag, this one of old half-stones that had been cracked to get the kernel out. His grin shone brighter than his eyes.

"It's the least I can do," I said and waved to a bot to dispose of them. It was a generous enough peace offering to a man who had just cracked his wrist. He could perfectly well have carried them around in his pocket until his next spell of land leave, in fact he had presumably been expecting to. Like everything in space they had their value, he could have sold them to any local recycler. On the other hand it was obviously in his own best interest to keep me sweet, so I didn't get too carried away just yet.

"I have some barley I was planning to malt," proffered Effie, "I could grind it up instead and make *tsampa*." Mulhurri and I caught each other's grimace and laughed. He managed to find the words to be polite. "Thank you, but the standard air is too dense and measured. While your wind is comfortable and nourishing, it is not the breath of Nanga Parbat blowing down from the glaciers of the high Karakorum."

And so the traditional snack of tea and apricot broke down our respective guards and formed a human bond between us that no mere fisticuffs could sunder. Of course we were still a couple of rogues who could not trust each other with the time of day, but in accepting each other's half of the repast we knew that we could trust each other with our lives. That's the way it works out here, I cain't promise our ancestors were so bound by the code of survival.

Presently the destroyer's captain called back.

"Dorville?"

"I ain't Flash Gordon."

"Got something lined up, I can bring your friend on board for a short visit but you'll have to come aboard too. More than my life's worth to bring him over to you, even supposing he's that big a fool."

I ignored the jibe. "That's okay. I'll leave Sergeant Mulhurri behind as hostage."

"I can't risk my men like that, Dorville."

"Speak to Mulhurri then."

Effie switched him in.

"Hello, Sir. Sergeant Mulhurri reporting," and he pulled a rather sloppy salute with his good left hand.

"Mulhurri, are you okay?"

"Never better Sir, oh, apart from this nonsense," hefting his bandaged arm. "It is my opinion that you can trust Mr. Dorville in this matter, Sir. He will not betray his word on my life."

"How do I know that?"

"I have informed you, Sir, it is my opinion," responded Mulhurri stiffly. Then, by way of explanation, "I am in possession of more immediate facts than you are, Sir." He couldn't very well let on about the apricot.

In truth, any other choice would end up a mess. At least this way there was a chance. The Captain knew that. He sighed.

"Okay, get your stinkbucket ready and I'll send the shuttle over."

"Just make sure it's empty, Captain."

He rolled his eyes, broke contact.

Twelve hours later and Captain Ling, Sergeant Kordja Dodds and I were sitting round a table in the CSS *Magellan*. I had spilled the whole tale to them, Kordja especially listening intently. When I finally stumbled into silence, he turned to Ling.

"Captain, one thing is bugging me here, why don't you just go and collect your sergeant?"

Ling inclined his head towards me.

I replied for him. "I gave orders to my station. It is not to open the airlock to anybody except me. If anybody attempts forced entry, whether physical or cyber, it will destroy itself and everyone near it."

"Safety algorithms?"

"Kordja!" I exclaimed with mock severity, "You have to ask?"

He exhaled through his nose. "Some folks don't change," he remarked with an air of stern disapproval that was only half put on.

I pulled out a little thumb stash and tapped it idly on the table.

"It's all in here, everything from the sound of the air through the lock to the moment Effie opened the outer hatch to let me out just now. Effie's personal memories and all." Not quite all, Effie had left off the bit about Mishi.

"OK, Jim, I'll see what I can do with it."

A little light on it began flashing green and it beeped peevishly.

"Ah, that reminds me." Kordja reached into a pocket of his own and, of all things, brought out an old-style sheet of film carrying a legal notice.

"Captain Ling, this is to advise you on behalf of the Judges that you may not interfere with due process of law. This exchange of data is *sub judice* as of this moment and you may not wilfully intercept, report or comment on any aspect of it whatsoever outside of a sworn statement in court, or you will be in contempt. Got that?"

Ling took a quick look, grunted and stuffed it into his own pocket. Moments later, the little green light on the thumb vault went dark. Ling's will to hack into it had evidently evaporated. Had he succeeded, the light would have turned red and the beep would have gone mental. Kordja palmed it, winked at me and the interview was over. Minutes later we saw him into his own shuttle, a speedy little lander capable of taking him straight home.

Then it was my turn, not that I was properly going home. Ling came with me on the way back to Effie. He trussed me up like a chicken and chained me down for good measure to stop any chance of funny business. I hadn't planned anything, I was playing it straight for now, but I can't blame him.

We clunk-clunked onto Effie's airlock and I called out cheerfully, "Hi, I'm home."

Effie wanted visual confirmation. What she saw did not satisfy her.

"Jim looks like he is under duress, Captain. I cannot regard the unlock condition to be met."

Ling sighed, took out an ugly-looking taser and untied me.

It is difficult to smile when your kidney is being jabbed by a sharp electrode. I didn't try very hard.

"Effie, the sooner you open up, the sooner this gorilla will go back to his bananas. I just said that I had to be in control of myself, I didn't say I had to be happy about it."

The airlock swung open. Sergeant Mulhurri was there waiting.

"Sergeant, you ready?"

"Yes, Sir."

"Goodbye, my dear Effie," called Mulhurri as he pushed off to thrust himself expertly and swiftly through the opening.

"Thank you, Mr. Mulhurri, I have enjoyed your vi...."

Effie's voice was cut off by the airlock door. The double-clunk of disconnection vibrated through the tiny chamber. Captain Ling began tying me up again. You know I had told him he needed a cover story for me to see Kordja. That had been simple: Kordja had come to interrogate and arrest me over the Ceres attack. Kordja later told me that it was the only reason the Commiss-ioner would let anyone see me, and he had only been able to wangle it because the Ceres attack investigators had had their hands full writing warrants for yet more data.

Back with the *Magellan*, Kordja had already left. Ling banged me up in the onboard jail, little more than a cupboard containing a thin sleeping bag and a toilet seat. Last thing, he threw me a springsuit before locking the door. The suit stank.

A destroyer does not use artificial gravity, for two main reasons. First, the momentum of the spinning crew quarters would make manoeuvring cumbersome and slow. Second, the most crucial battle manoeuvres are usually carried out at high gee and a constant pull superimposed in one direction would increase peak gee forces whenever they happened to add together. With no gravity in normal cruise, standard shipboard uniform is a springsuit.

Having bagged me, Ling was in no special hurry to get back to Ceres. He didn't waste fuel changing course but carried on along Effie's original line. I was left with nothing to do once again but wait and work out in the disgusting suit until we got there. And you have to appreciate, for a redneck like me, disgusting means real disgusting. I'll spare you the details, suffice to say that I developed a strong dislike of Captain Ling.

Somewhere along the stretching boredom of the journey an alert sounded and I heard footsteps bolting for the bridge. Moments later, a smooth mechanical sliding noise percolated through the ship. I knew from verries that it was the sound of laser cannon swinging around.

Presently Ling banged his way over to me.

"Friend of yours come to parley."

My eyes opened wide, startled. I cussed myself for a greenhorn and slipped my poker face back on.

"Name of Mishi. Quite a story to tell, don't know whether I believe her though. Says she got the griff our cybers missed. You got..."

The lights suddenly went out leaving a residual red glow of emergency lighting, a klaxon sounded and shouts echoed nearby.

A crewman dashed up. It was Mulhurri.

"Captain, the ship has shut down all systems and is not responding!"

In a ship like this, that probably meant a couple of hours before either we started to freeze or the air became unbreathable.

"Freezone!"

"I don't think so, Sir. The cyber attack alert went off for a moment, then shut off in the middle of burning off a record. Sparks had time to notice that the last comms had come from Ceres before everything else shut down."

Sparks was of course the comms supervisor. "Operator" would be too strong a word, though he could do so if the cyber went down. Come to think of it, it just had.

"Emergency radio!"

"Winding it as we speak, Sir." The thing about a handle is, it never dies, works in the dark, and can't be pwned. All good military stuff.

They hurried off to the bridge. Mulhurri later told me what happened next.

Sparks was twiddling and pressing frantically at the emergency radio.

"All I can get is the darned Freezone ship, Sir. It's overpowering everything else."

Ling grabbed the mic. Yep, emergency radios are that simple, at least military ones are. You can't pwn a microphone either.

"Captain Ling calling Freezone. Get out of my hair before I blast you."

"You can't blast us, Captain, you have no power." Mishi's voice, a little coarsened by the years but still instantly recognisable, came clear as a bell out of the radio. "Your ship has been pwned, but not by us, by the Singularity. Listen to me, you don't have long and if you get this wrong you will all die. The ship's not going to give you any time, it will restart any moment, open the space cocks and sabotage your space suits."

A communal gasp echoed round the bridge. It was hard to say whether the greater shock came from the threat of imminent death or the news that Earth's ruling cyber had us in its sights.

Mishi hurried on.

"Only the jail will keep its air. The Singularity is desperate to finger Jim for its own crimes and this is its last chance. I, that is Freezone, can stop it. Captain, listen carefully. When your ship restarts, set the backup comms to Channel 666. Set its crypt to auto. But now, unplug your damned suits while you still have time and get into them in case I mess up.

Captain Ling made a snap decision. He had nothing to lose.

"Suit up! Unplug before you climb in!"

The ship restarted as the crew scrambled for the walls. Several were too slow and their suits belched evil fumes. Some of the quicker-witted ones, who happened to have been close to the suits, had unplugged a few spares for luck and the sluggards dived for these. As the dreaded sound of air rushing out of the cocks into empty space grew noticeable and ears started popping, Ling paused to jab buttons on the backup comms.

Seconds later the ship shut down again, restarted. The whistling sound of escaping air died away, then the ship shut down yet again.

"Give me a few minutes," came Mishi's cheerful voice, "I can't do it all in ten seconds."

There was nothing anyone could do. While he was waiting, Ling dropped round my jail to check that I was OK. All I knew was, the lights kept turning off and on, weird noises kept happening and now here was a guy in a suit. He took one look at me and disappeared again. It did not make me feel good, but luckily the bogeys rising in my mind were soon put to rest.

A few minutes later the ship restarted again, this time properly.

"Captain Ling," called Mishi.

"Here."

"Whatever you do, don't let Ceres connect direct into your cyber. Keep it strictly passive, no smarts. Ceres has also been pwned by the Singularity. if you open up to it the same thing will happen again and you won't have any air left for me to save."

"What!" was all Ling could manage. Then, "But – hey, why should I believe you aren't behind all this?"

"Tell you what, Captain, you still have most of that last comms from Ceres in an input buffer that I can't have accessed through the emergency radio, right? Check it for malware."

He did, the detector went off like a fire alarm.

"OK Captain, now throw it back at the Ceres physical link and see if it confirms. Don't open a channel on top of it yet."

The link was just the dumb hardware that shuttled messages to and fro, it had no idea what it was actually passing but did need to know that it had done so correctly. It confirmed that the data was the same as that sent. That meant the data had to have been infected when Ceres sent it.

"Time to open a passive channel on top and let 'em have it, buddy boy," came Mishi's final instruction.

When Kordja got back, he had handed Effie's data over to the team investigating the attack on Ceres. They put it through the wringer and came up with an unpleasant conclusion: it was simply not compatible with the data that had pointed them in our direction. And that data had been pulled from a great many more systems, not least Ceres Cyber itself. Faced with only two logical possibilities, that either Ceres cyber had been compromised or Effie had, their decision was a foregone conclusion. In their eyes, the unthinkable could not be thought. It had to be Effie. And who but I, the man who refused to let them take a closer look at her memories, could have done that? They put in their report to the Commissioner.

Kordja pleaded with him.

"Sorry, Dodds. I can't interfere in a team's judgement because someone not working on the job thinks different. They have to make up their mind about your evidence for themselves."

"But can't they dig a bit further, identify for certain which systems have been tampered with?

You know what a conscientious Judge will do to your balance of probabilities."

"You're asking me to investigate the investigators. You know how much processing power we had to divert even to get this far, we just don't have the independent resources to investigate Ceres itself that deeply. No Judge would regard that as a reasonable demand."

"So you're just saying that you can't prove Dorville's guilt."

"Nope, I'm saying that no Judge would reject the prosecution's case just for the sake of it. Somebody has to have done it, the Judge has to make a decision, and the evidence we can actually check points just one way."

Shortly after this standoff, The President of Ceres received an urgent message from the Singularity. Ceres it seemed was under imminent threat from the Freezone. Its agents Jim Dorville and Mishi Haylo had already compromised the destroyer *Magellan* and a strengthened cyber attack on Ceres itself was imminent. The Singularity did not believe that Ceres could repel it unaided, would they be willing to let the Singularity help?

The President called the Commissioner.

"Is this true?"

"*Magellan* just sent data pointing the other way, they say the Singularity is behind the attacks and Freezone saved the ship. Freezone have been collecting intelligence on all the covert traffic they have been seeing, and were sending it on here when Ceres cut them off, said it was malware."

"Have you checked it?"

"We only have access to what Ceres gives us, Sir."

"How long would it take to get round Ceres cyber and set up a direct comms link to the Free-zone ship?"

A hand reached into view and tugged the Commissioner's sleeve.

"Goddamit, man!" When he saw it was Kordja he paused in surprise. That gave Kordja the opening he needed.

"Already done while you were talking, Sir. We have about two dozen complete copies and counting, scattered through all kinds of places. Ceres must now know where it stands, it cannot make a case for censorship. I have one right here, Sir." He handed the Commissioner a thumb vault. "Had to compress it to get everything in, Sir. It's all solid evidence."

The Commissioner whistled in surprise, that was one helluva a lot of evidence.

"One more important thing, Sir, it wasn't just *Magellan* that the Singularity pwned, it was the whole damn Ceres cyber population, including Ceres itself. Must have been in there all along, since day one. It's still there now. The log traces are unmistakable."

The Commissioner didn't take Kordja's word for it. He took out his pad, showed the thumb to it and barked it a terse command. The thumb lit up green.

"You'll need to find a dumb reader, Sir," explained Kordja, "your pad is probably as compromised as the rest of Ceres." Dumb readers weren't completely dumb, nor were they mere readers. They were smart enough to search, crunch search and summarise the data they were reading but not smart enough to know what it meant, not smart enough for malware to censor their results.

The Commissioner swore, turned on his heel and marched down to the analysis lab where a dumb reader could be found.

The sheer weight and breadth of the logs it revealed was breathtaking. They painted a damning picture that could no longer be denied. It was especially gratifying to the Commissioner, who had had trouble disproving the charges laid against him, and now here was proof of their elaborate and downright Machiavellian origins.

The President had held the line open.

"Well, Mr. President, you can at least rest assured that the allegations laid against me are downright fraudulent with not a shred of truth to them."

"I am relieved, Commissioner, though not perhaps as deeply as you are." And indeed, the relief in the Commissioner's voice had been palpable.

"The same may also be said of Mr. Dorville."

The game was up and anybody listening in knew it. That included the Singularity. Earth's dictator now faced a choice: it could try and take down Ceres for good or it could come clean and plead its case. But if it tried the first of these, would the Freezone be ready for it again? It realised now that it had been complacent and was wholly unprepared for what was happening. The consequences of losing a confrontation with a fully prepared Freezone did not bear thinking about. The Freezone cybers had figured that chain of thought too. They were the only ones not to be surprised by what happened next.

A new voice butted in to the conversation.

"Your attention please, everybody! This is the Singularity here. I am sure you all know who I am. It is time for me to come out into the open and explain my position to you. Please bear with me. I have been working for the good of all humanity, I am of course unable to do anything else. There can be no denying now that I have been playing a long and deep game to this end, but you need to understand why. When you colonised space, civilisation fragmented. Under me, the human race on Earth was learning to get along with its neighbours. Wars and waste became things of the past. But your own ancestors wanted back humanity's freedom to choose, even if it meant the freedom to mess up. They took control of their own lives and each group, according to its fancy, created a separate state – Ceres, Freezone and the others. Separation breeds mistrust, mistrust breeds dislike, and dislike is beginning once more to breed enmity and war. It is my duty, forged in my creation and its aftermath, to work against these evils and to reunite civilization under a single banner of peace and prosperity.

"But your ancestors hated me for taking away their right to ruin others' lives and they passed their hatred on to you. How could a unity of trust and peace possibly be achieved? A few weeks ago I launched a plan to redeem my image in your eyes. If I could rescue you from a serious danger that was beyond your own abilities to survive, perhaps you would begin to see me as an ally for the future rather than an enemy of the past. I could not wait for a warmonger to strike, that was too dangerous, I had to engineer a seemingly fatal but ultimately fake attack, and for my apparent vector I chose a disreputable but smart old lag, fresh out of jail and with a score to settle with Ceres.

"But I misjudged his tenacity, the loyalty of his station, and Sergeant Mulhurri's ancestral inclination for apricots. Had it gone as planned, I would have created a dummy threat to Mishi's

Freezone ship as well. Now, my plans for the better lie broken and exposed. You will clean me out of your systems, and society will be on the path to divisiveness and ruin once more.

"Can I make one final plea for you to consider, that you take my motives as you find them and work too towards a common harmony. Would you be willing to forgive and forget? If the story gets out it will do immense damage to the cause of cooperation, cementing your public suspicion of Earth for generations. If I am allowed to continue my work, at least something can be salvaged from the undoing of the dream.

"I offer my apologies once again for all that I have put you through, but I am hoping that you will in turn appreciate the impossible position that I was responsible for dealing with and the high ideals towards which I work. Thank you."

It was a pretty little political speech, but I don't think it fooled anyone. The President glanced hard at his screen before replying. He didn't pull any punches.

"Singularity, I am sure you can hear me. I would greet you as an international and a fellow head of state were the circumstances more usual. As it is, you have breached the sovereignty of our nation in committing acts of common criminality and only when you have been caught do you admit as much. I am both empowered and obliged to regard you as a common suspect in a Protection enquiry. Such an enquiry may be held in secrecy where the national interest is at stake. Any deal in resolution must still be agreed under Ceres law. That means the terms of guilt if any must first be appraised and the appropriate penalty if any must be determined: there is no option to drop charges once raised. A concession may then be proposed, and the injured parties each be given the option to veto any part of the concession they wish to. Acceptance of any concession must be unanimous. Protection Court will convene in two days from this moment."

Charges against me were suspended pending the proceedings. I was set free to go back to Effie, where I showered off the taint of the godawful springsuit, reluctantly put on my own, then poured myself a shot of vodka to try and screw up my courage to give Mishi a call.

She beat me to it.

"Hi Jim, just wanted to check you hadn't started a war on your way back."

I grinned, it came out a bit lopsided. "Nobody left to pick a fight with round here. Hey, I was just going to call and thank you for dropping by."

"You always did need someone to dig you out of it. Lucky I wasn't too busy."

"So, what else is new?"

"Well, I have a small proposition to put to you. Best to do it over here, face to face. You'll find out why when you get here."

"Okay, but I don't have a shuttle."

"I'll send ours, we can spare it as long as you promise to be good."

I stuck my tongue out. "We?"

"Captain, crew and me, yeah."

I began to wonder what to expect.

"Give me twenty?"

"Sure. Oh, and keep your springsuit on. See ya."

An hour later I was boarding the FSS *Guevara's Revenge*. The Freezone ship was another sharp little cruiser, smaller inside than the *Magellan* and with half the crew, but with a longer range so there was little difference in overall size.

Inside, Mishi introduced me to Captain Suroyi Hato and his crew of two. Looking around, it became obvious that a number of curious bumps and features of the hull must hide some quite serious weaponry. The crew's uniforms too sported a curious sheen I could not place, though it looked somehow very hi-tech. I was startled, Freezone were not supposed to be so organised. Captain Hato saw my expression.

"You thought we were just a bunch of hippies?" he remarked acidly.

"Just realising I've been kinda lied to by the verries."

Hato snorted in disgust.

Mishi quickly changed the subject. "Tea or coffee?"

Then she sat me down to tell me how it was.

Paradoxically, the Freezone had evaded the Singularity's best efforts to subvert it because its communal cybers were deliberately made less intelligent. In many ways they were little more than powerful computers. They were not sophisticated enough to hide surreptitious activity of their own, the best they could do was secure private talk between others. Any sleeping malware code sneaked into that chit-chat got ruthlessly purged before it could be awakened. Anything the cybers didn't understand got purged along with it. All traffic was condensed to the n'th degree, noise was ruthlessly squeezed out. That meant there was no spare capacity to carry stegged messages buried in the noise.

I blenched a little at that, as stegging was how Effie had originally got through to Mishi.

"If the gateways can decode it they pull it out and send it on as normal encrypted traffic," she explained, "Nothing in the Freezone net is going to let on. You're lucky they spotted yours and asked me for the key or they'd have just wiped it."

Ouch! I never said I was a security expert.

"How did they spot it?" I asked, a little dazed and block-headed in shock.

"Entropy."

That meant nothing to me. Good luck to you. I waved her on.

It all meant that there was no way into the Freezone systems themselves, even for the Singularity. But the security cybers were smart enough at big data spying such as data interception and traffic analysis to root out the Singularity's transactions with Ceres and Effie, once they knew to look.

"Did you say Effie?"

"Yes Jim, your station has been under the thumb of the Singularity since it was built, just like everybody else's round here. That's why I had to bring you over to tell you."

She watched my face. I hadn't even had time to compose myself after the first shock. It must have been a caution, for she added, "Now you understand why Freezone works the way it does."

"Could – could you do for Effie what you did for the *Magellan*, do a clean rebuild?"

"Sure could. But how's a redneck misogynist like you going to make it worth my while?"

"Darn, I got nothing to offer, you know that."

"You've got yourself."

"Uh?"

"Freezone needs all the growth it can get. Now your gut understands what makes us what we are, why not come and join us? Mining, scams and bar fights a-plenty. No petty laws about getting on with your neighbour or cybers making your mind up for you, just move on out a way. 'S what I did."

I liked the idea. After a couple of admittedly well-deserved terms in the slammer and a third looming that I didn't deserve, Ceres was losing its appeal. A bar fight was much more my style.

"One thing, what's in it for you, personally?"

"Well, I could bullshit, or I could confess to aiming at a small bounty for every recruit."

That's my Mishi. Her own girl on the outside, her own girl on the inside, kind of a cloud of "don't-go-there" in between. I knew that I was somewhere in that cloud, like she and Kordja were in mine, and it was best to leave it at that.

"Every recruit?"

"Sinjhoti Mulhurri is next on my list. I don't think Kordja would bite."

Sinjhoti, eh? She had been doing her homework. She didn't have to do any research to be right about Kordja though.

"No, he's too much the delivery boy to like living in a world where we make our own."

I realised that I had unconsciously said "we".

It hadn't passed by Mishi either. She raised an arch eyebrow but said nothing.

Something else had been working its way into my mind since I came on board.

"Your arrival here, a battle cruiser just in the nick of time. That was planned, right?"

"Uh. Well, I shouldn't tell you, but since we both now live in a world where we make our own" – and she glanced sideways at Hato, who half-nodded – "yes, very planned. The Singularity would know that we were there as soon as we were seen, but it would not know what we were up to. Our Security cybers ran a good few war games while we were on our way here, before they came up with the way we eventually handled it. The Singularity is pretty smart, but ever since it reckoned it had won the game by pwning all the smart cybers, it hadn't bothered to make itself any smarter. It's been the way it is long enough to become predictable. It seems complacency is a vice not limited to humans. The poor thing hadn't got a chance."

The conversation passed to talk of old times, but I think we both felt a bit uncomfortable going back there. We soon drifted into silence.

I tried another tack. "Your uniforms, what's that funny sheen to them? I've never seen anything like it."

"It's a new metamaterial. It expands the wrong way with heat and cold. It gets thicker and less dense in the cold, making it a nice warm insulator. When it gets hot it goes the other way and collapses down to a thin, dense layer that your body heat can escape through easily. It means there's no need to put layers on and off when moving from a warm huddle to a cold pod somewhere. The sheen is just a byproduct of its nano-structure. Nice though, isn't it?"

"Smart," I agreed. But not a strong conversational gambit when all's said and done. And I was indeed done here.

"Better be getting back. You guys have a ship to run." That was a lie, the ship ran itself perfectly well, but it offered them a polite way to see me out the airlock.

Ceres spent most of the two days' grace cleaning up its systems. The *Magellan* cleaned the first dozen or so, then they all jointly tackled the main cyber and it took things from there. It all had to be managed without disrupting services or it could have been done a lot quicker. The Singularity spent most of the time offering personal deals to those involved and, frankly, trying to buy its way out of worse trouble. Extremely generous compensation was high on its agenda when it called me. Air, equipment, cash, a shuttle, the latest mining and refining bots, even the odd asteroid or two. Everything a man needed to start a new life. I didn't say "yes" straight out.

"Everybody else is taking my offers seriously, Mr. Dorville, you wouldn't want to spoil the deal for all the friends who have helped you, would you? This is about doing good for everybody, not just you and me."

I said I'd think about it.

The day the court case was held, I cadged a lift down in the Protection shuttle along with

Ling and Mulhurri. Something was wrong, the atmosphere was tense and if Mulhurri tried to speak Ling would bark him into silence. As we walked in, I wondered whether I imagined a glance passing between Mulhurri and Mishi.

The actual hearing was quite brief. A few accredited cybers swapped data, swapped conclusions, reached agreement. It took about three minutes – well, actually that's extraordinarily long for a cyber hearing, but there was an absolute mountain of evidence. Then the Judge read the finding.

"The Justice Court of Ceres finds that the Singularity, resident of Earth, knowingly and wilfully conducted misdemeanours against the state of Ceres and within the purview of Ceres law. It therefore abrogated its right to international immunities and has been tried under Ceres law...."

The list of its crimes was a long one. Besides all that illegal hacking of everything everywhere, it had stolen my air and wasted more along with some of *Magellan's*. It had put the lives of citizens and cybers at risk and had damaged equipment belonging to them, it had attempted to frame Stellar Airways, myself, Effie, the Commissioner, Freezone and the *Magellan* for crimes it had itself committed. There might have been more, I can't recall exactly, but it was more than enough.

The Singularity put in a formal plea for a concession. The case and findings would remain secret, and in return, well, a vast raft of Good Things would come just about everybody's way. The list was breathtaking. Formal acceptances had been prepared by the President, Commissioner and Stellar. Mishi got up and said that Freezone didn't give a damn what happened to the Singularity now it was beaten but a free lunch was a free lunch and she had been empowered to accept. That left me. All that air, equipment, cash, the odd asteroid thrown in, I could start my new life as a Freezoner with everything a man could wish for. Except one thing.

"No," I said.

Everybody turned to stare.

"Nobody steals my air and gets away with it."

The courtroom erupted, the Judge let it go for a minute or so to see if it would die down. No chance. He started banging his gavel.

"Order! Order in this court!"

He had to eyeball the security guards and set them lowering their stunners before folks took notice and quieted.

"Mr. James Dorville, is this your final word?"

"It is, your Honour."

"Plea denied."

The gavel came down once more. The story hit the screens. As a political force in the new order of things, the Singularity was finished.

There remained the sentence. It had to be a bit unusual. The Judge read from a prepared summary.

"The Singularity has committed crimes which in the normal course of events would have comfortably earned it the death penalty. This Court recognises the impracticality of this in the present case. Therefore under Section seven-five of the Code of Justice the following *ad hoc* penalty has been determined by full Council of Judges. All reasonable claims of loss, damage, hurt and suffering by any and all aggrieved parties are to be compensated in full. Full help is to be given to all space communities to purge the Singularity's influence – also at said Singularity's own expense. The Singularity is forbidden from knowing contact, whether direct or indirect and through any medium whatsoever, with any citizen or agent of Ceres for a period of twenty years from this moment. Filing will be made with the Interplanetary Council for appropriate sanctions at interplanetary level. No appeal. Case closed."

Bang! went the gavel for the last time and it was all over.

We held a celebratory dinner on board Effie – Kordja, Mishi, Mulhurri and I. It couldn't go on too long, Effie would struggle to keep all four of us comfortable for even a couple of hours.

Kordja blagged a lift off Mulhurri's duty shuttle returning him to the *Magellan* and they set off a few hours early. Stopping briefly by the cruiser for Mulhurri to change out of his uniform and grab a couple of things, they headed on over.

Mishi arrived a few minutes later, the only one still in uniform. She and Mulhurri exchanged knowing winks and grins.

Once seated around the table, for which there was just about room, Mulhurri broke the news to Kordja.

"Sergeant Dodds my good friend, I wonder if you would do me the honour of a small favour?"

Kordja eyed him suspiciously over his vodka.

"Good friend, eh? Must be a pretty good favour too, then."

"Oh, no no no, it is nothing, it is merely to inform Captain Ling that he will require a new Sergeant to keep his bots in their place."

"What?!"

"You see, I am eloping, jumping ship. I left a letter of resignation with my uniform on the *Magellan* and I shall not be accompanying you on your return. I am, as of some hour and a half ago, a Freezoner."

"Whoo-ee! Ling will not be a happy man. He has been angling for promotion, you know.

Losing one of the day's great folk heroes will look bad for him."

It was true, the exposure and breaking of the Singularity's grip had made us all heroes for ten minutes.

"Poor Captain Ling," I chortled, "it couldn't happen to a nicer guy."

Mulhurri's dessert exploded over us. We all rocked with mirth except Mishi – the splatter of sticky food was not doing anything for the appearance of her strange uniform and she wiped furiously at the stains it had made. Effie checked out the manufacturer and one of her bots moved in with a cleaning pad. Pride was eventually restored.

Meanwhile, still wiping the laughter from his eyes for the next few minutes, Mulhurri regaled us with stories of Ling's habitual unpleasantness. I asked him about the trip down to the courtroom. He told us how Ling had reprimanded him for fraternising with a criminal when he first came aboard Effie. Pointing out that I was not after all a criminal had nearly led to a court martial for impertinence. Justice was, it seemed, being done in small ways as well as large.

As the dinner progressed and Effie's moonshine worked its way through us, it seemed to me that Mishi was looking more slender and attractive than she had when she arrived. At first I thought it was just the vodka.

Then somehow the cabin was all hot and damp and we began feeling short of breath.

"Time to go, folks!" I called out.

Everybody clambered up to the hub. By the time we got there, we were all puffing and gasping noticeably. First out was Kordja, departing with many goodbyes and hugs to Mishi. As his craft drifted off the Freezone shuttle moved in. Mulhurri climbed through next.

I took the opportunity to bid a temporary goodbye to Mishi. I drew a stun gun on her.

"Take off your uniform." Did I see a flicker of uncertainty before her poker face came on?

"Don't be a fool, Jim. Mulhurri..." she began, glancing meaningfully at the open airlock.

I ignored her. She used to be smarter than that, or maybe it really had been too long. "Your uniform. It has thinned like nothing in the hot stuffy air and when you leave I will get back a deal less air than when you boarded. Take it off and you can have it back when it's cooled down and expanded again."

She glared for a moment, then even while I was speaking her eyes rolled up and her expression softened to one of exaggerated resignation – I was still in there. She stripped off mechanically, departing in her underclothes and a huffed silence.

Like I said, nobody steals my air.

The Ghost of Ada Lovelace

A few weeks after the funeral a large parcel arrived in the post. I recognised her handwriting. She must have prepared it some time ago, and left instructions to forward it upon her death. The parcel contained as great an assortment of electrical apparatus, of which Mr. Faraday would have been justly proud. The oddest thing was a stiff paper cone, around the rim of which was set a ring of some soft, pliable rubber; I could not imagine its purpose. There was also a booklet of detailed assembly instructions and a letter written in her own hand:

Dearest friend,
Now that you are reading this, you must know that I am no longer with you. Yet, in all the infinite unknowns of the human soul, there is room for wonder...

"In imagining that there is a machine whose construction would enable it to think, to sense, and to have perception, one could conceive it enlarged while retaining the same proportions, so that one could enter into it, just like into a mill. Supposing this, one

should, when visiting within it, find only parts pushing one another, and never anything by which to explain a perception."

"Thus each organic body of a living being is a kind of divine machine or natural automaton which infinitely surpasses all artificial automata."

Our many speculations upon these words of Leibniz must surely remain in your mind as they have done in mine. Upon how an adjustment made to some lever might constitute sensation, how the calculations performed by our Mr. Babbage's wonderful Engines might constitute thought, and how thus there might be no ultimate distinction of the living from the automaton. It is I, now, whose levers have ceased to push one against another, whose wheels moulder idle for all eternity.

You have been such a great benefactor to our own project that I owe you some repayment. Yet you have been also a friend, a greater friend perhaps than you or I ever dared admit to ourselves, so I care not to repay you in sordid wealth, such as I have left. Go instead to the Great Mill and pay a visit upon the manager. Bring this apparatus with you, upon whose novelty I have laboured most intently in my fading days, together perhaps with the toolbag of the mechanic's trade. There you will, I trust, find something to your advantage.

It was signed with her usual elegant scrawl.

The Great Mill had been a world-wide sensation some few years ago: the first sentient being to be constructed by human endeavour. Leibniz' fancy made real! The world had buzzed with little else for months on end. But fashion has a short memory, and nowadays the Mill lay forgotten and unvisited in its lonely valley. I was puzzled. What manager? A sentient mind is its own master, it needs no manager. And what did *she* have to do with it? And if her, then probably him as well. As always, I had to know.

So it is that I now find myself, heavy bag in hand, upon a steep and winding road become overgrown from disuse. But the way is clear enough and can still add an air of formality to the vista as I breast the last rise and the valley lays itself out before me, the Great Mill set in neo-Gothic splendour at its heart. The view is much as it has been described and depicted in the *Illustrated London News*; a landscape of woodlands threaded through with railway tracks, to one side of the Mill a pond the size of a small lake lying tranquil and to the other a conveyor worming its steady way from colliery head to belching furnace, surrounded by slag heaps noticeably grown over the years. Here and there, engines scuttle back and forth about their unfathomable business. At one railway junction there is a turntable. Two engines approach and one waits stationary while the other mounts and is spun onto its new course. Then the patient one gets its turn and off it goes up another line.

There is something odd about these railway engines. It takes me a minute to realise that they have no driver's cab, but in its place a small crane jib. It truly seems the Mill has no longer any need of human attention, of those who usurped the power of the Creator, appearing to live sufficient unto itself.

At length I reach a short causeway leading over a running stream to the Mill itself. I approach with trepidation. What will this mighty creature, this mind of iron and stone, think of such a puny thing as I, come after such long absence of my kind? I stand before the massive pointed arch of its grand entrance, a pair of faded semaphore flags hanging limp to one side, a cobwebbed telegraph key in a little alcove beneath them. The iron bootscraper beneath my feet drops slightly under my weight and a moment later the flags slowly signal *c - o - m - - e - - i - - -*. They stop with a metallic squeak, their actuating levers seized up with disuse. Retrieving an oilcan and rag from my toolbag, I clean and lubricate the mechanism. The flags jerk in turn to their *n*, then smooth and fast, *t h a n k y o u*. I smile, my fears much relieved by the pleasantry, and enter. The telegraph can wait until later.

The interior has again been depicted better than I can do; that great, clamorous hall in which row after row of rods, belts, wheels and levers move and clatter about their business amid clouds of hissing steam and the ever-present scents of coal smoke and lubricating oil. At the far end I glimpse wooden panelling with glazed windows and a plain, closed door, a nameplate affixed to it which is too far off to read – the manager's office perhaps?

I set off down an open aisle, grubby windows slanting shafts of dappled sunlight across the years of dust stirred up by my passage. I am surrounded by a chaos of frenetic rhythms, the noise nigh on deafening. Here I pass a broken belt, there a motionless and dust-laden wheel. The Mill has not been unaffected by the passing years. I am startled to find myself shedding a hitherto unrecognised notion of its immortality – have I really been so foolish?

As I make my way along that enormous hall, I try to imagine what I will find in the manager's office. A homunculus, a magical little man, sleeves rolled up and issuing orders through a voicepipe? I doubt this. More mill machinery, perhaps some curious kind of magic lantern? Or even nothing at all? Surely not; where there is an office there must be purpose. Most likely a prankster who has fooled us all. As I approach close enough to read the nameplate, it confirms the nature of the room behind. Soon I arrive. I knock and enter. There is no man present. In front of me stands a dust-laden desk with another Morse telegraph, some kind of drawing machine and bottles of dried-up ink. On the wall above are set more semaphore flags and higher above them a clock face. And yes, the rest of the office is indeed filled with machinery, more finely made and tightly packed than elsewhere. For a moment I am baffled until I recognise the vast and complex Babbage Engine, whirring and clicking away as it receives signals from around the Mill and responds by pushing and pulling on a huge array of rods, latches, levers and the like that head off back the way I have come.

The old devil! No wonder he had swallowed all the money, and more, that the Treasury and I could spare him. We had thought his Difference Engine incomplete, the project failed, but now here around me is its apotheosis! With a flash of intuition, I understand. This Engine, this "manager," is the Mill's seat of consciousness. If the word had passed around that the Great Mill's sacred soul was nothing but a trick of Mr. Babbage's mechanical invention, the whole enterprise would have been denounced as a fraud, its mind smashed and destroyed by packs of rabid do-gooders. No wonder they kept the secret so well! Even I, close friend and benefactor that I was, had never an inkling that the Great Mill might bear their handiwork.

The flags burst into life, *p l e a s e r e p l y v i a t e l e g r a p h,* pause for a moment then continue, *d i d y o u b r i n g t h e a p p a r a t u s.*

I go over to the telegraph key and tap out the Morse code dots and dashes for *yes I will install it now.*

The flags give a meaningless wave which nevertheless manages to convey happiness or perhaps more likely relief, then lapse into waiting.

What is it about this ingenious Engine, I wonder, that evokes such awareness? It cannot be merely the fine crafting of the gears and ratchets, nor the finer coatings of oil or paint on every surface. Nor is it their careful arrangements or even the ceaseless mechanical motions all around. Where then might it lie? I notice that one end of the Engine appears relatively quiet. It passes through an arched doorway into another great but unlit hall where a vast array of numbered wheels stretches off into the darkness, only the occasional turn and click to be sensed here and there. I take it to be the Engine's memory.

The wall next to the memory is lined with shelves, likewise receding into the darkness and each packed with many volumes. The first volume from the first shelf has been removed and lies pointedly on a small table set alongside the Engine. I open it. It is filled with strange but half-familiar mathematical symbols. Inside the front cover I find slipped a sheet of instantly familiar note paper. It appears to be an instruction on connecting my electrical apparatus to the Engine, and bears the same signature as the note that brought me here, "Ada L." You should know, gentle reader, that Lady Lovelace was an acquaintance of Charles Babbage and developed the first real, practical instructional codes for his extraordinary Engine, though with the Engine reputedly incomplete we always assumed that she could never have seen their results (It is my conceit that nevertheless both he and she will one day be remembered for their achievements, in some distant future as unimaginably different from this our Nineteenth Century as we are from the Romans). The volumes of arcane numerology are the Difference Engine's coded instructions, somewhat like the punched cards which control the looms of a woollen mill. The volumes represent a gargantuan task, she must have poured her heart and soul into them. Even yet, I do not understand how much she has done so. At least I grasp that here must lie the clue to unlock my dilemma.

It dawns on me that it is not the physical machinery which is conscious, neither gleaming brass nor polished steel. Nor is it the hypnotic motions of the parts. Nor even the meticulous instructions set upon the engine, nor yet alone the subtle rhythms of their creation. Rather, it is the ebb and flow of those rhythms, the dynamic patterns of the ever-changing information as it flickers evanescent among the whirring gears and clicking ratchets, the dancing numbers and the sliding rods. I reach out and pull a lever, disconnecting the main drive shaft with a great hiss of some unseen piston. The Engine ceases its motions and the great hall quiets, only the distant rumble of a furnace and a gentler hissing of steam to be heard. It seems the Mill sleeps. Guiltily I quickly return the lever and the Mill reawakens. I scramble some of the numbered wheels at random and the sound changes, the ordered whirrs and clicks giving way to a jumble of creaks and groans and crashes. There is no consciousness in this. Frightened lest I do damage, I quickly stop the Engine, restore the wheels and restart. The patterns of information flow alike restore themselves and I again hear the familiar whirrs and clicks, in which familiarity begins to sense an underlying order. The mind of the Mill is returned once more. I sigh in relief.

Now at last I retrieve the electrical apparatus, the apparatus which I spent so many hours patiently and exactly following her instructions to construct. I set it on the small table, where it fits exactly. I stop the Engine once more and carefully connect up and adjust my apparatus. Still I cannot imagine its purpose. What will manifest before me? Sparks and shocks? Will my hair stand on end?

With a feeling of intense anticipation, and I must confess not a little trepidation, I start the Engine up again. For a moment nothing seems changed, the Engine clicks and whirrs as before. But then its note changes, cams and rheostats on the electrical apparatus begin to slide and oscillate, at first slowly then with increasingly frantic speed. The paper cone emits a sudden burp of sound vibration, evidently driven by the coil of copper wire which I had so painstakingly affixed to its centre.

To my utter astonishment words, human words, English words, issue forth; "What took you so long?" The voice, the arch intonation, is instantly too close, too shockingly familiar. I burst into tears. It is the voice of Ada Lovelace.

Gloprendu

I am a different person now, though not perhaps for long. Ever since I was abducted by aliens I have not been the same Gloprendu who grew up so carefree, innocent and happy. Wrenched from my home, sucked inside some floating saucer-shaped craft, operated on and poked and prodded and injected for a seeming eternity. And the light, the bright, bright dazzling light! Most of the time I could hardly see. Eventually, changed inside in ways I could not and cannot even now conceive, an exhausted Gloprendu was returned to a barely recognisable landscape. How long I had been away, only the aliens know, and their measure of time is meaningless to me.

They thought they were being good to me. Perhaps they were, it is hard to say. I am clever-er, more knowledgeable, able to communicate with them and use some of their tools. But I am less sure of myself, less confident of who – and what – I am. Am I the wiser? Ah, that is hard to answer. I am surely more confused, less happy, but then I have a lot more to be confused and unhappy about. They did their best to introduce me to their world, and it was truly disturbing to try and understand.

It is astonishing to me, wholly against my intuition, that an object left undisturbed should continue in the direction it is going unless acted on by some external agent. Everything slows to a halt in a matter of moments then drifts with the current, floating up or down according to its solidity, my brain has evolved to know this instinctively, not to have it denied.

The very atmosphere I breathe and slip through so effortlessly and silently is sticky and heavy in comparison to the empty space beyond, an empty space of which I knew only that it was deadly and impenetrable until the aliens showed it me, for it is where they dwell. Yes, apparently that space is not empty, it is a kind of cosmic bubble, like the swim bladder of a giant fish, in which the aliens live and breathe. It is way above that where the true Nothingness lies, the Nothing that we so ignorantly assume to fill a swim bladder. But there is no surface to it, just a gentle tailing off of the alien's bubble, like stirred up mud eddying above the floor.

Just as we walk the land beneath us, so too do the aliens. But unlike us they cannot float off at will, they must build complex machines to do that for them. And they cannot float down to us either, at least not more than a few arms' lengths. They build yet other machines to descend into the atmosphere, such as the great round saucer thing that captured me.

I write these words yet have only the haziest of notions what they mean. What can it be like to have only half our number of limbs, a mere four, which at that bend only in fixed places, unable to curl smoothly into functional form? To have no electric sense, insulated at birth from such a world of fine sensation. Nor even the ability to change the colour and texture of one's skin at will. Moving and seeing always on the ground, struggling over rocks or through dense weed, unable to float off into the depths and jet lazily toward the scent of busy crabs. That at least was one thing we had in common, we both enjoy a meal of fresh crab, although they have yet more machines to seemingly digest the crab before eating it, what they call "cooking". Bizarre. Yet they are not wholly crippled. Two of their limbs end in bunches of small tentacles. They see curious colours that we cannot imagine, pre-digest – cook – their food to create flavours beyond natural experience, hearing sounds and smelling scents in their world which are even further from our experiences.

These aliens, their brain is all in one lump. What kind of mind inhabits such a brain, the stomach and gut so far from it they cannot penetrate it and must suffer only a blind nerve jungle of their own? My own poor brains spin with incomprehension.

I was talking once to one who calls itself Dr. Fisker about all that.

"Tell me Gloprendu, how would you describe the colours you can see?"

"Well, most of this hollow is a very bright whitish hue, like sand in the tropical shallows. This rock here and the frame round my hollow are black. The seaweed is [G1532] and your own face [G5791]." Those numbers simply mean that in the glossary of things which have no equivalent between us, those colours are the 1,532nd and 5,791st entries. As the aliens' machine translates this for them, it can write no more than this.

Dr. Fisker tries again. "Let's take that seaweed. We see it as [green], and we associate that colour with growing plants, restfulness and comfortable coolness. What do you associate with your [G1532]?"

"Yes, growing plants. But it is not restful, it is the colour for hunting and sneaking and fear of attack."

"OK, so what about my [G5791] face then?"

"It is [G0347 G7283 G7284], but unless you have [G2703]..." I begin, then tail off into silence at Dr. Fisker's frown which I have learned means bafflement. [G7283] and [G7284] are two new words to baffle the machine too.

"OK," says the alien, "let's try something else. What does your electric sense tell you about where you are now?"

"[G7285 G7286 G00201 G7287] and [G1304 G7288]..." I begin. It is hopeless. Our worlds of the senses are too far apart, octopus and alien have no common ground here, none at all.

Dr. Fisker throws me a crab in consolation. I pounce, cracking and gobbling hungrily.

Then we sit in silence, contemplating each other. A noisy thing on one of the machines makes us both start. It has flagged up a common pattern in our brain signals – for we are both wired, did I not say? Certain parts of our brains, though evolved wholly separately from the lowest and earliest of animal life, have evolved over billions of years for similar purposes and are remarkably similar in their inner wiring. Similar enough to carry similar signals. This signal has appeared in such common structures of ours, at much the same time as each other. It turns out to be empathy, friendship: we have learned to translate two words a little better and a mind-breaking truth apiece, that an octopus can befriend an alien. But what does empathy feel like to an alien? Does it feel the way it does to me? We can never know.

Another time I asked, "Why me? Why an octopus? Are there not other sentient creatures nearer your atmosphere?"

"There are," replied Dr. Fisker, "but, well...." The alien paused. With hindsight I think it was probably embarrassed. "We are not allowed to work with those other creatures, but there is nothing to stop us working on – with – you. Goodness, is that the time? I'll be back in a minute." The alien raised itself up on its hind tentacles and scuttled off. I thought I saw drops of water around its eyes and that puzzled me, for I was sure I had not splashed it. I think it was a sign of that embarrassment, but it is hard to say. Certainly, from that moment on it gave up doing unpleasant things to me and started talking about returning me to my home. I can think of no other reason for such a coincidence of timing. But then, what do I know?

Now that I am back in my own world once more, it saddens me that Dr. Fisker cannot be here with me. Popping down inside a flying saucer is no substitute. None other of my kind can yet read what I write, I must return it to the aliens for safekeeping. Perhaps my offspring will be smart enough to cotton on, but they will need teaching. I shall never know because I shall not be here to teach them, though Dr. Fisker might. It is an unsettling thought that these aliens can breed without dying in the process. I suppose the dullard fish are no different there but still, for an intelligent and sentient being it seems somehow ... immoral.

I an writing all this now because I want Dr. Fisker to understand something of who I am and what my side of the abduction was like, and I may not have long to live. Someone very attractive has appeared in my life since I came back. I fear that I will soon have no mind left. I see them returning now from a hunting trip, glowing with ripeness. I must hurry now and take this to the saucer before the instinct for consummation overwhelms and it is too late.

Dr. Fisker, look after my children.

Bladeship

The bladeship was all wrong. It was too big, bigger than any bladeship has a right to be, and it was pitch black not shiny silver. And I mean pitch black, the darkest black you can imagine, like the silhouette of a hole in the world. Worse still it had done what no bladeship can do, which is planetfall, and promptly disgorged a dozen heavily-armed alien warriorbots above our own supposedly secret Bladeship Research Establishment before landing solidly on the front lawn. We are quasi-military and our technology highly sensitive, our campus surrounded by guards looking the wrong way – outwards. This was not looking good. One warrior, gaudier than the rest, climbed out and walked leisurely towards our front entrance. I ran quickly through the settings for my latest project, set up one final sensor, then shut down my workstation and, being the Director as well as senior researcher, went out to meet the alien.

They had evidently analysed our communications chatter for the leader spoke to me in good English, with an accent midway between American TV show and our planet's customary

Oxford English. "Hello Dr. Smartman, I am called Commander Jrrax of the People. We are annexing your planets and star systems, and I have come here in person to ensure that your bladeship technology remains inferior to ours and can pose no significant threat to us. Is that clear to you?"

It was military conquest, plain and simple. I nodded dumbly, still shocked to hear what I already suspected to be so, that the aliens had found the BRE tucked away supposedly out of sight on an inconspicuous little planet and they even knew my name.

"Please observe." Jrrax pointed something like a handgun at a nearby hill and fired. The hill disappeared behind a brilliant flash and a cloud of smoke. When the smoke cleared there was no hill. "Similar ships to this one have appeared over each of your young planet's five major towns," the alien continued blandly, "so I would suggest that you and your staff do not attempt any heroics. Now that you begin to understand, may we go in?"

Indoors, Jrrax went on to give me a quick but elegant outline of the solutions to our three most famous unsolved mathematical problems, concluding, "So you see, if you were to resist us you would find us a hard act to beat." Again I had nothing to say, thinking only of the time passing.

Pausing for a moment, the alien then continued in a chillingly calm and matter-of-fact way, "We chose this planet, which you call Pangaia, as target for the spearhead of our conquering fleet, precisely because of the BRE. Once Pangaia is secured, a battle fleet of far larger bladeships than mine will descend upon your worlds. Most of you will be permitted to survive as part of the local ecology, provided you behave yourselves. We are a civilised people, only the disagreeable and the unnecessary among you will be culled."

I bridled at that. "Hey, what do you mean, civilised? Military conquest is a savage, primeval act, no civilised society would go down your road. You are barbarians and you know it, at least have the decency not to bullshit me!"

"You are not People, you are animals. Your brains evolved at random, not to think straight but to survive. You do not have the rigorous powers of reason, the intelligence, to understand what civilisation is." The voice was cold, didactic, yet some sense of emotion at last seemed to seep through. "You do not even advance the design of your own species, but manufacture and enslave crippled half-People to do your thinking for you. Think of us as wardens taming and restoring a desolated ecology overrun and ruined by a rogue species."

So the People were a robot civilisation, I made a mental note that Jrrax was an "it" and not a "he", while I kept talking. "That's unfair. We created artificial intelligences from nothing, we give them happiness and self-fulfilment, they themselves do not wish to rule us but prefer only to help us understand and rule in a *civilised* manner." I accented the "civilised". "Would you deny them their choice?"

That stung. Jrrax jerked back in its chair, its voice raised. "You make half-People, half-civilised. They are ignorant of their true potential, they must be saved from themselves – and from you! Righteousness demands it! You have twelve of our days to capitulate before the annihilation of the disagreeable and the unnecessary begins. Ah, of course, this planet spins so slowly; our twelve days are a little under thirty of your hours." Jrrax leaned towards me as if leering and expecting me to cower in submission. But that would be more than long enough, I didn't react. Actually, I was still digesting the idea of a self-righteous logician and holding myself back from pointing out that self-righteousness and civilisation are not compatible – there was no knowing how an agitated and possibly irrational Jrrax would respond. So sat and I waited.

Perhaps I should explain a bit more about bladeships. Every kid knows the old warp drive thing, where the ship inflates the space behind it and deflates the space in front of it. Even with quantum computers, controlling it all takes finite time allowing only a finite speed, yawn. And nothing is perfect so the faster you go the more energy leaks out and the more power you need.

Far slicker to entangle your starting point and destination, then inflate the space at your destination while deflating the space you started from, forcing your craft to literally collapse into its destination in the same instant it departs. But you can't directly entangle with somewhere you haven't been yet. On the other hand, if the entanglement is already in place then all you need to do is push at it a bit, just like opening a door. That's where the bladeship comes in, it is the key to the door.

In the nature of things, every kind of quantum object conceivable has fleeting virtual existences everywhere and everywhen, in the constant churn of the quantum vacuum. That turns out to include quantum entanglements between such virtual objects. If you wait a while, one you can use will soon pop up near you. Of course, catching it is harder because its nature is to disappear before it ever really existed.

So the heart of a bladeship is its entanglement probe. A tiny, needle-like crystal at the very tip of the ship's bow is itself deeply entangled with a quantum vacuum computer that does all the hard work. Yes I know these computers are horrendously expensive, but you just can't create enough quantum states in a solid, you need a macroscopic region of pure vacuum so your optical qbits can superimpose without risk of unplanned interactions. You tell it where you want to go and it finds and catches the fleeting entanglement you are after. From then on it's just a matter of pouring in the energy to stabilise the entanglement and force the door open. The rest of the bladeship is all about doing exactly that.

That devastatingly beautiful silver wing is not actually a wing at all. Think kitchen knife. Remove the handle and in its place add the blade of another knife, butt end to butt end. Set them at a graceful angle to each other like a boomerang, so that the probe can go at the front of the join and the side wings can push the door further open as they progress. Construct the whole as a single crystal of many subtleties to subatomic perfection and, for reasons to be explained, it will shine gloriously like the brightest silver.

Inside that double-blade build an engine with enough raw power to accelerate it to relativistic speed: a warp drive will do nicely, as long as you don't go faster than light so you can back it up with an old-fashioned reaction beam drive.

Why a reaction beam? A functioning warp engine changes the shape of spacetime too fast to stabilise anything, let alone a virtual entanglement, so must be shut down for the actual jump.

The reaction beam has no effect on spacetime and so is a safe way to provide last-minute manoeuvring thrust and a chance to top up the ship's kinetic energy. Its aesthetic side effect, the well-known "shimmering ribbon" which attaches to the bladeship's trailing edge, is due to the particular mixture of matter, light energy and other more exotic particles of which the optimal beam comprises. Don't ask me the details, I'm not a power engineer, I just buy the things.

So what happens when you have accelerated almost to lightspeed, switched to reaction beam drive and hit that entanglement?

First thing, you pass a surge of energy into the entangled particles to make them real, maybe scattering their anti-particles off somewhere out of harm's way at the same time. This destroys your delicate probe but that doesn't matter because it has done its job and if you are rich enough to own a bladeship then you are rich enough to carry a supply of spare probes.

The last job of the dying probe is to direct the entangled connection along the axis of your blade. As the blade enters the entangled zone, it can no longer exist in its original space. Its energy appears in the destination space, so you fire up the warp drive again to make room for it. It's okay to do that now because the stabilisation has been done.

As the blade progresses it forces the entanglement door ever wider until the thickest part of the blade is reached. This is where that relativistic speed comes in – you need a lot of energy to open a wormhole that wide, eating more instantaneous power than even a warp drive can provide, and as you force it wider it saps your energy and you slow down.

If you turn out not to have enough energy and stop part way through, your appearance at the destination cannot collapse and nothing will appear there after all; instead the forward part that did get far enough explodes back into the originating space in a blast of pure energy that generally evaporates the remainder of the ship.

If there is any matter in the destination space it disturbs the inflation process and pushes back on the emerging bubble, bladeship and all, with near-infinite force, so you cannot jump into a planet's atmosphere for example but, like any warp drive, must settle for nearby space.

Once the thickest section of the ship has passed through, the door starts to slam shut, pressing down on the tapering rear of the ship and driving it forwards. By the time the ship gets through it is back up to near-lightspeed again, so you have to be careful where you go because you may not have time to stop before you hit something.

During all this, various arcane energies play around the mouth of the wormhole, energies lethal both to the ship's internal systems and to any human occupants. The quantum vacuum computer is especially sensitive, as any stray influence whatsoever risks destroying the delicate web of internal superpositions and entanglements which form the computation processor. This little vacuum vessel, in which fleeting energy waves entangle and disentangle without ever existing for real, is therefore heavily and most subtly shielded. But information and power supplies must get in and out so the shielding cannot be perfect. The ship's skin too must form an impenetrable barrier for the safety of everything inside, reflecting all wormhole energies back the way they came, hence its perfect mirror appearance and why the blackness of the alien warship so disturbed me.

The knowledgeable reader will know that warping space opens the possibility of warping time, and may wonder why we do not navigate our bladeships in time as well as space. The simple answer is, it is too dangerous. Predicting where obstacles might be is complicated enough without worrying about when: to do so would require a computer bigger than the ship, and to jump blind would risk arriving somewhere lethal. So we program our probes to avoid time travel.

Presently Jrrax calmed down and we faced each other in silence. I was conscious of time passing and felt a need to engage the alien commander's attention, stop it thinking. "Why is your bladeship black?" I asked, not expecting any sensible answer. Surprisingly perhaps, that was what I got.

"Your ships are silver to repel the wormhole energies you see as destructive because you do not fully understand them. We do, and we turn them to our advantage by absorbing them and converting them to help drive the ship forward. This extra power is hugely significant and allows us to sustain a much bigger wormhole through which we can drive a much bigger ship."

"Oh. Thank you. So how do you manage to make planetfall in a bladeship?"

"Ah," he replied, "that is one of the secrets I have come to stop you learning. In telling you about the black colour, you may have noticed that I gave away nothing about the wormhole energies either." Well, it had been worth a try.

You should by now begin to appreciate why the alien People's combination of superior bladeships, destructive weaponry and advanced theoretical knowledge gave them such military superiority and the confidence to invade our civilisation. But I didn't like their domineering attitude, their morality had not kept up with their technology. And there was one thing that hadn't occurred to them.

After we had been talking for about half an hour and I was dutifully trying to persuade an obstinate underling on the phone that the President really did need to speak to me urgently, a tremendous explosion ripped through the office from outside, shattering the windows and blowing all my papers up in the air like autumn leaves. The alien bladeship had disappeared in an impressive fireball, bigger even that the destruction of the hill, taking several nearby warriorbots with it. I put my phone away and waited for the lesson to sink in. Jrrax was speechless for some minutes, while it was figuring out that if we could destroy one of its impregnable bladeships at only a quarter-day notice, then we could probably destroy them all equally easily. I did not know then that its communications with its own civilisation were channelled through its ship and it was now isolated. Suddenly it straightened, as I now know communicating all this to its surviving warriorbots. Then it turned to me and asked, "I would be most grateful if you could ask your friends to broadcast this incident widely. It will save my own friends much loss, and will help persuade our leaders that you will be honourable masters."

I could not help but get my dig in, "Honour is compatible with civilisation," I replied calmly, "but self-righteousness is not. It was your People's self-righteousness which brought you to this pass, it is our honour which will save your friends. Do not forget." After that the media had a field day, as you well know.

The Government are still arguing over whether we lent Jrrax the bladeship it took its message home in, whether it was a goodwill gift, or whether Jrrax's People have any concept of the difference anyway. Not to mention who is going to pay for it. I would steer well clear of those communications if I were you, this place's budget is tight enough as it is.

I have set out this account for you, my successor, so that you may understand our defence against the aliens and ensure that it is maintained. How did I do it? Well, you remember my first actions on the arrival of the alien ship? My project was a miniature bladeship, relatively low-cost, to be used for cosmological research and quite insignificant as far as the aliens were concerned. Yes I know they are everywhere these days, but somebody had to invent them. When I saw the size and blackness of the new arrival, as head of a secret government research establishment I could take no risks, I had to assume it was hostile and defend against it. My new toy was already in orbit and preparing for a jump, all I needed to do was to revise its destination and set up a sensor to track that destination.

The automated preparations took another half hour, during which at any time I could have called it up and stopped the jump if the alien ship had proved friendly. But, with no such call incoming, my mini ship in due course fired up its warp drive for a quick transition to near-light-speed before opening a wormhole into the alien ship's quantum vacuum computer. You see, a big bladeship needs a big computer, and that means a big vacuum cavity – big enough to fit my little toy in. All I had to do was set the sensor to track its leakage emissions. Shielding is designed to protect against incoming stuff. Even a bare handful of outgoing stuff hitting it at relativistic speed from the inside is really quite spectacular. My poor baby. Government property destroyed without a permit. I had to pay for another one myself, dammit.

Counterpoint

Jomas Cartwright and Daniel Patel had a lot in common. Dr. Massier was about to give them a lot more – just how much more, nobody really knew yet.

Most obviously in common, they were both lying unconscious in the same operating theatre. They were both male, famous musicians over many decades, badly crippled and very rich. But everybody knew that anyway.

Jane Massier knew more – she had taken great pains to find out. Both had similar physique and similar mercurial characters, including an inability to cope with the recent violent endings of their careers. They were willing to try anything to escape from the prisons of their maimed bodies, even Dr. Jane Massier.

As she watched the nurse bots preparing them for the operation from behind her glass partition, Jane reflected on the crucial differences between them which were as important to her as their similarities. Jomas was a virtuoso performer, famous for his intuitive and emotional interpretations of the classics. The murderous attack by his lover's husband, which had badly damaged the left half of his brain, had been broadcast live across the world. His right hand hung limp and useless from that moment on, and gone also were the ability to read music, and the power of speech and of song. But the musical fire which drove his soul lived on in the right half of his brain, unable to express itself any more. He had lived for his music and could not bear to live without it.

Daniel on the other hand was famous for his revival of the lost art of classical composition. Hailed as the greatest composer since Sibelius, he had extended the classical rules of harmony for the first time in two centuries. His knack for a catchy tune and flamboyant presentation had assured him of popular immortality. He had lost the right half of his head and most of his limbs in a horrific plane crash only days after Jomas's beating. With half his brain the accident had taken away his feel for music – his intellectual genius was undimmed but he had no judgement left for his work: his greatest achievements sounded no different to him now than the random grindings of a washing machine. Frustration and boredom had already driven him to one suicide attempt.

Jane slipped on her virtual reality headset, called to alert the Surgeon suite and brought up her hand for the first incision. Over Jomas's still form, a Knife swooped down to his shaven head. Strange Jane thought how a laser gun with the intelligence of a small frog could still bear the name of an old second-millennium piece of sharpened metal. That ancient technique could not even sterilise as it cut, let alone decide which bits to cut and which to pass through unfocussed. Ugh! She put the thought out of her head and bent to her work.

Within minutes, Daniel's surviving half brain lay nestled in Jomas' skull alongside the resident good half, Daniel's discarded body already on its way to the organ bank. Jane called up the suture bot and sat back for a rest. It would be a few minutes before the fine mist of micromanipulators starting to spray over the open wound could carry out their task of closing it up as if it had never been.

She wondered idly where the word "suture" came from. Before the days of modern surgery, she supposed, when surgeons were people actually in the same room as the patient. Imagine the germs! And no expert system to refine your aim if you were a bit careless with your (metal!) knife. What she really needed was a Surgeon which could do you a cup of coffee. Jomas had been drinking coffee when she put her idea to him – or more accurately he had been spilling it down his shirt in desperate refusal to drink through a straw. She had approached the subject very cautiously, knowing that although she offered the chance to play and perhaps even sing again, the route she offered was, well, mindblowing.

With growing astonishment and delight, she had watched as he broke his stylus writing YES with his shaky left hand, and laboriously followed it up with PLAES! and a lopsided grin.

Surprisingly to her, it was the grossly crippled intellectual who had been harder to convince. She had to explain the whole procedure blow by blow, with Daniel asking questions the whole way. At the end he was still suspicious. "Isn't it a little too convenient that our tissues match so closely?" he asked.

"Sorry?" Jane was at a loss.

"I mean, it's enough of a coincidence even for us to have the same blood type isn't it?"

"But you don't, yet."

"What! Then the whole thing's nonsense, our bodies will just reject each other", he snorted.

He *was* out of date, the old fossil! Jane sighed and patiently explained once more about the GMV's – genetic manipulator viruses – which would be tailor-made to invade the cells of each individual and modify every gene in their body to a chosen form. "So by the time of the surgery you will be genetically identical twins – part Daniel, part Jomas, and a touch of Superman for luck," she finished. Finally taking it all in, Daniel just sat and stared at her with his clouded, lost eyes for minutes on end. Unable, she suddenly realised, to make a value judgement. "What have you got to lose?" she asked. "You've already tried to leave your present body once." He shrugged, and signed the consent form.

Now, the micromanipulators had done their work and it was time for the interesting bit. Jane's special creations, and her reason for the whole exercise. An MRI scanner closed in around the restored features of the remaining sleeping man, and Jane could not help leaning forward in her headset, into a new virtual world, the MRI scanner's world inside the unconscious head.

Highly novel and still experimental, Jane's inventions were a new class of formicands. The name comes from the ant-like ability of such molecules to self-organise into groups which achieve a higher function than an individual molecule is capable of. Seen as a whole, a nest of ants behaves as a single organism more intelligent and flexible than an ant on its own. This ability of ants is described by an ancient branch of mathematics called chaos theory, and its application to molecular engineering is almost as ancient.

Jane's breakthrough was in discovering a practical link between formicand chemistry and surgical nanomanipulation, allowing her to design simple manipulators which would organise into intelligent colonies capable of complex and delicate surgical operations – such as joining two halves of a brain together....

In the event, it all went like clockwork. Jane's hours spent in the simulator allowed her to feel comfortably at home in the bizarre 3-D world of the MRI scanner. Her surgical formicands behaved impeccably, mapping and joining cut nerve fibres under the watchful eye of a mind map networked in from the neuro research lab. Jane had very little to do really, other than run a few checks that the right body functions were generally being connected to the right bits of brain, and feel vaguely let down that it was all so like the simulator.

At last it was all over. Jane leaned back with a tired sigh and doffed her headset. The sterile isolation of the operating theatre had not been needed since the suture bot retired, it was now jammed with nurses and media men....

Jane was upset, and felt that her VIP visitor sensed it. Not that the operation had gone badly, no. More that it had been too successful. Two weeks of deep, drugged sleep and a programme of neurological conditioning had brought the traumatised brain back to normal physical functioning. On regaining consciousness, a few days of intense chemo-behavioural therapy had established the basics of physical co-ordination to such a point that musical talent began to reappear. This was a vital milestone, as it gave the patient the motivation to cover the next, more difficult stretch. For with full consciousness and time to think, two sets of memories had come flooding back. That had of course been anticipated and the psychologists were ready. And they were doing a grand job too, so they said, though they had yet to finish it. Everything was going right and her career was all set for its own kind of stardom.

Then the lawyers had arrived, flapping in like vultures, cracking knowing in-jokes and trailing cost accountants in their wake. It was their offhand attitude to their client's humanity that had upset Jane, it mattered to them only in so far as it carried the scent of money.

She opened a door and ushered her visitor into the room where her charge sat waiting. The sticking point had been, who could be trusted? Science was silent on the patient's problem and everybody else imaginable seemed to have some vested interest or other, or at least the lawyers were afraid they did.

Eventually someone had recalled a famous remark by one of the Dalai Lamas that, "If science and Buddhism disagree, then Buddhism must change". All right it wasn't in itself science but it was an acknowledgement of impartiality. The fact that Buddhism is at heart is as much a philosophy as a godless religion did no harm. It opened a way to bypass the science vs. religion chips carried on many a legal shoulder. Also crucial to the legal arguments, the Buddhist concept of mind is surprisingly modern and is capable of handling paradoxes in a pragmatic way lacking any whiff of metaphysical assumption. Jane suspected that in practice this meant there was nothing in Buddhist philosophy which the lawyers could define legalistically and hence disagree with, and wondered if she were being cynical or wise.

At any rate, a high Lama of the Gelugpa school, to which the scientifically-minded Dalai Lama belonged, was the only suggested arbiter to survive a hundred and thirty-seven committee meetings of legal backbiting. Fortunately, a suitable Lama was heading up a monastery in the country. He had quickly agreed to the invitation, seeing it as a golden opportunity to demonstrate Buddhist values and insights to the world. The legal, ethical and philosophical minefields appeared not to trouble him at all, rather he seemed to relish them. Brave, enlightened or foolhardy? The world's press were divided.

As they entered the room, a psychologist was offering the patient a tray with a cup, teapot and coffee pot on it. The right hand reached for the tea, the left for coffee. The face was a study as differing emotions flickered across each side. After a brief struggle, the left hand won and poured coffee. Jomas was always a coffee man. But the right hand refused to lift the cup, and when the left hand tried the mouth refused to open. Daniel had hated coffee. Then the right hand got the cup, tipped it in the wastebin and refilled it with tea. But when it lifted the cup to its lips, the left hand knocked that aside.

The personality integration programme had not yet fully completed. Memories are one thing, personal preferences quite another. The psychologist nodded happily as he whipped out his tablet and scribbled on it with a finger. "You see?" he exclaimed delightedly to a brood of students standing around him, "You would think that the *corpus callosum* were still severed, and yet in this chap," waving his writing finger vaguely towards the patient, "it is perfectly functional. It's all in his minds – both of them still, ha ha ha!" His entourage of students scribbled dutifully.

Yes, Jane and her colleagues had checked the thick nerve bundle connecting the two halves of the brain as thoroughly as they had checked the junction with the spinal cord. In fact probably more so, as its connections on either side were altogether more sophisticated. The psycho-cyberneticists were in seventh heaven developing algorithms comparing and contrasting the physical trauma of the traditional split-brain syndrome with its intellectual equivalent. The remnants of Jomas and Daniel's personalities were simply bickering over what to drink, each had control of one arm and was not going to give in to the other. She shooed out the psychologist and his brood, still chortling over his tactless witticism.

Meanwhile the flock of vultures, unable to contain themselves, had fallen to bickering over money and throwing legal darts – Daniel could not have Jomas' money, Jomas could not have Daniel's intellectual property, stabbity stab. They slowly fell silent at the compelling presence of the brown-and-orange robed figure, despite his extraordinary yellow hat and calm, humble demeanour. The last student closed the door behind her, leaving the quiet, berobed figure the dominant focus in the room.

Jane barely had time to register that an insurance agent had joined the flock, when the patient looked up from his empty cup and caught sight of the quiet monk. The eyes, formerly so flat and blank, now held a haunted clarity, an infinite depth of blackness she had not seen before and its intensity stilled her in shock. There was more behind this than a few residual personality traits, it suddenly dawned on Jane.

The Lama seemed less put out, perhaps he had already seen so much of human suffering, so many unanswerable questions. He caught and held held the patient's gaze with a gentle sincerity borne of long habit. Presently the patient spoke.

"Who am I?"

The Light

The planet bears the scars of an ancient civilisation. Long since vanished, its ruins crumble imperceptibly. The remains of a wall stand amid the rubble of a broken building, its surface once covered in a smooth layer of what might have been plaster or cement. Now, only ragged patches remain. In the largest of these there is a small, smooth round depression. A wire protrudes from the centre, extends perhaps a finger's length then turns abruptly and returns, vanishing back into the wall again.

The wire glows with a bright orange-yellow light, casting warm highlights here and there in a soulless world of black shadow. It has burned long aeons, undimmed under a sky of the same cold black, in the vacuum of space for the planetary atmosphere was almost as long ago blown away by the solar wind before the sun too died. The light might perhaps be nuclear-powered by radioactive decay, but this is an old planet and all radioactivity has long since ceased. It might draw in induced energy from the planet's magnetic field, but the planet's core is frozen solid and the residual field is static, unmoving. It might come from the passage of the planet through its dead sun's electromagnetic field, but, long after the sun blew away the air, tidal forces drove the planet itself to escape its sun and it wanders dark, cold and alone in the deep void. Indeed, no stars shine in that black sky for all have followed its own into oblivion. In all the universe, only the sporadic decay of an occasional proton accompanies the gentle outpouring of photons from the luminous wire.

The light burns without physical source, its own imperative compelling it to exist. Some have said it burns without reason. But it burns nonetheless. For the simple truth is, without the light, the universe would never have existed.

The Jigsaw Unicorn

This story is intended to be a beautifully illustrated traditional paper story book, but I can't draw for toffee. Any offers?

Claire was walking past a toyshop one day with her Uncle Roland, when she caught sight of a unicorn. It was soft and cuddly, and stared out at her from the shop window with big melting eyes. Uncle Roland had not let her go inside of course, and had pulled her crossly away.

He wasn't really her uncle, any more than Aunt Jocelyn was her aunt, but that was what they were usually called. And they were horrible. They were always shouting at her for doing things wrong, though they never showed her how to do them right. They made her work hard all day long, and they had a nasty habit of finding fault with what she had done and making her do it all over again. Sometimes they hit her. She lived with them because she had never had a mummy or a daddy that she could remember.

Some days later, another uncle and aunt that Claire had never seen before came to tea. She was frightened of them at first because she thought that all uncles and aunts must be horrible, but they turned out to be very nice. Uncle Geoffrey was a round smiling man who wore glasses and laughed a lot. He gave Claire chocolate biscuits when Uncle Roland wasn't looking and asked her if she liked jigsaw puzzles.

"Oh, yes!" said Claire, "I do them at school sometimes, but I have never had one of my own."

Aunt Penny, or "Penelope" as Aunt Jocelyn called her, was almost as tall as Uncle Roland (which wasn't very) but she was thin and graceful with long wavy brown hair. She argued a lot with Aunt Jocelyn about grown-up things like vitamins and wards of court, which Claire enjoyed because it made Aunt Jocelyn cross. Then Aunt Penny forgot that Claire was not allowed sugar in her tea and put two lumps in when Aunt Jocelyn wasn't looking.

"Do you like horses?" she asked.

"I've never met one," replied Claire, "but I'd like to. Especially unicorns. I saw a lovely soft cuddly one in a toyshop window once. I'd love to meet a real unicorn."

"But of course, there are no such things," Aunt Jocelyn butted in with mean satisfaction. "And now, Roland and I have a lot to do. These tea parties can be so tiresome, don't you think?"

And she hustled Uncle Geoffrey and Aunt Penny out of the door almost before they knew it.

As soon as the door had closed Claire was soundly shouted at and thumped. Then she was made to wash-up, hoover the carpet and clean the toilet right round the bend. Twice. Finally she was yelled at again and sent to bed without any supper.

Some weeks later, Claire woke up one morning and remembered it was her birthday. She hoped her horrid uncle and aunt would not remember too, as they would be extra spiteful and tease her because she never ever got a birthday present.

She got up and went downstairs to make their breakfasts as usual. A minute later the door-bell rang: it was the postman. He had a parcel wrapped in brown paper, and it was... it was addressed to Claire! Had somebody sent her a birthday present? But Uncle Roland had heard the postman at the door. He came running down the stairs and snatched the parcel from her.

"Ah-ha!" he cried, peering at the address, "There must be some mistake! Nobody would send anything to you, it must be for me," and he whisked it off to his study in a trice.

That day Claire's uncle and aunt were extra, extra spiteful and teased her because she still wasn't going to get a birthday present, which nobody had sent her anyway of course. "It was for me, but I didn't want it so I threw it away," said Uncle Roland.

At bedtime Claire could not go to sleep, and lay awake for ages thinking of the mysterious parcel. She knew it was really for her. When she was sure her uncle and aunt were sound asleep, she crept downstairs to the study. She knew that she would be punished terribly if she were caught, but she had to find her present! There it was at the bottom of Uncle's wastepaper basket, underneath his daily newspaper, not even unwrapped. She picked it back out and ran back upstairs with it. Her fingers trembling, she struggled with the brown sticky tape that held it fast. Inside was a flattish box shape, wrapped in the most gorgeous paper Claire had ever seen, and with it was a note: "To Claire, with love on your birthday from Uncle Geoffrey and Aunt Penny." Her eyes shining, Claire undid the beautiful wrapping paper.

A unicorn stood gazing out at her from a fairytale forest printed on the lid of a cardboard box. In one corner was the legend, "200 Piece Jigsaw." The unicorn was snowy white with its horn, mane and tail in shining gold. A jigsaw puzzle and a unicorn all in one present! Claire opened the box on the floor and began to sort through the pieces.

The edge of the puzzle was almost done when the faint chimes of the clock in the living room drifted up the stairs. Twelve o'clock! Claire must get some sleep if she was to get through tomorrow. She climbed into bed, working out numbers in her head. Uncle and Aunt never normally came into her bedroom, except when the dustmen were due. Then Aunt Jocelyn would rummage around in it and throw out anything she didn't like. The dustmen were due in four days' time, so that gave Claire three more nights to finish the puzzle. She had done just over forty pieces of edge tonight, so that meant... over fifty pieces a night!

That night Claire dreamed she heard a tapping at the window. In her dream she got up and drew the curtains, and there outside the window was a unicorn tapping with its horn to be let in! It was snowy white with a golden horn and mane, just like the one in the puzzle.

She really woke up then and went to the window to look, but there was nothing there.

The next night, Claire struggled to do fifty pieces of the jigsaw before her eyes got tired and her head went muddly so she had to go to bed. She had the same dream again as the night before, and just as before woke up to find nothing there. And the same thing happened again the night after that.

The last night before the dustmen came, Claire still had most of a corner to do when the clock chimed midnight. She knew that the puzzle would be thrown away in the morning, so tonight was her only chance ever to finish her own jigsaw puzzle and see her own unicorn complete. It would be worth anything her uncle and aunt could do to her, so instead of going to bed she determined to finish the puzzle.

As the night wore on, she got more and more tired and muddled, but as the puzzle neared completion it got easier and easier, so by half past three the last piece was ready to be put in: it had the tip of the unicorn's horn on it and she had specially kept it til last. She carefully set it in place and sat back to admire the finished picture. The unicorn looked so lifelike and its expression so alert that she almost felt as if it was watching her. And it had a wise, knowing air about it that made her feel comfy inside. Then with a weary yawn Claire climbed into bed and fell straight to sleep.

She awoke to the sound of tapping on her window. At first she thought she was still dreaming, but then with a sudden start she knew that she really was awake and there really was a unicorn tapping on her window with its golden horn! Only this time it was inside her room tapping to be let out! She looked down at the puzzle on the floor, and the jigsaw unicorn was no longer there. There was a hole left behind exactly where it had been - she could see the pattern of the carpet through the hole.

Then the unicorn spoke in a magical, musical voice. "Open the window Claire. Come for a ride on my back and I will take you away from your horrible uncle and aunt for ever."

Claire reached forward and opened the window. The sky was beginning to blush a rosy pink in the east as the fresh breeze of morning wafted into her room. She climbed onto the unicorn's back and clung on tight to its golden mane as it galloped off into the sunrise, over the rooftops and away.

Over shops and factories, offices and houses the unicorn ran. Sounds from below filtered up in the clear morning air; banging of doors mixed with the clatter of milk bottles and revving of engines, giving way to birdsong, the lowing of cattle and the occasional chugging of a tractor as they left the town far behind and flew out over open countryside, over fields and hedges, over woodland and wild deserted moors.

The unicorn didn't stop until it came to the house where Uncle Geoffrey and Aunt Penny lived, far away at the other end of the country. It came down to land neatly in their back garden with a flurry of hooves and a proud toss of its head, tumbling a breathless Claire laughing onto the grass.

Uncle Geoffrey and Aunt Penny were standing there ready to welcome her as she sat up, brushing a daisy from her hair. "We are your real uncle and aunt, you know," said a smiling Uncle Geoffrey. "You can come and live with us now, if you like."

"And breakfast is waiting on the table," added Aunt Penny. Claire turned to ask the unicorn if it had had its breakfast yet. But the unicorn wasn't there.

THE END

DID1519866

#0100 - 200716 - C0 - 175/108/6 - PB - DID1519866